VISUAL DICTIONARY

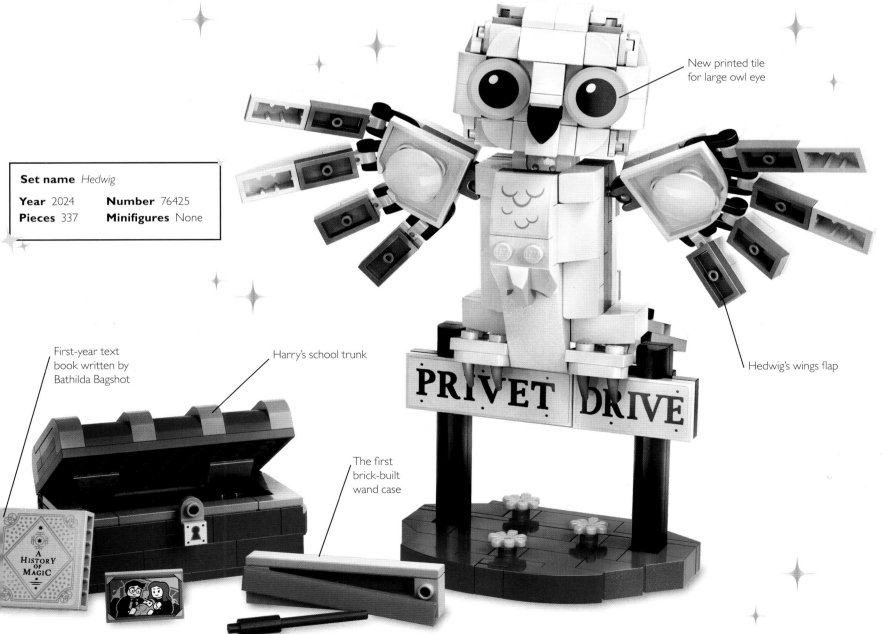

Set name	Hedwig	
Year 2024	**Number** 76425	
Pieces 337	**Minifigures** None	

New printed tile for large owl eye

Hedwig's wings flap

First-year text book written by Bathilda Bagshot

Harry's school trunk

The first brick-built wand case

PRIVET DRIVE

Dementor
microfigure

Headmaster's
tower

Hungarian
Horntail dragon
on the loose

Great Hall

VISUAL DICTIONARY

Creepy Dementors patrol the castle after Sirius Black escapes from Azkaban

Evergreen trees surround the castle

WRITTEN BY
ELIZABETH DOWSETT

CONTENTS

Scarlet and gold mid sections gradually increase in size

Turning the handle moves the wheels

Train can roll along tracks or be held in place

Track is 46½ in (118 cm) long

HOGWARTS CASTLE

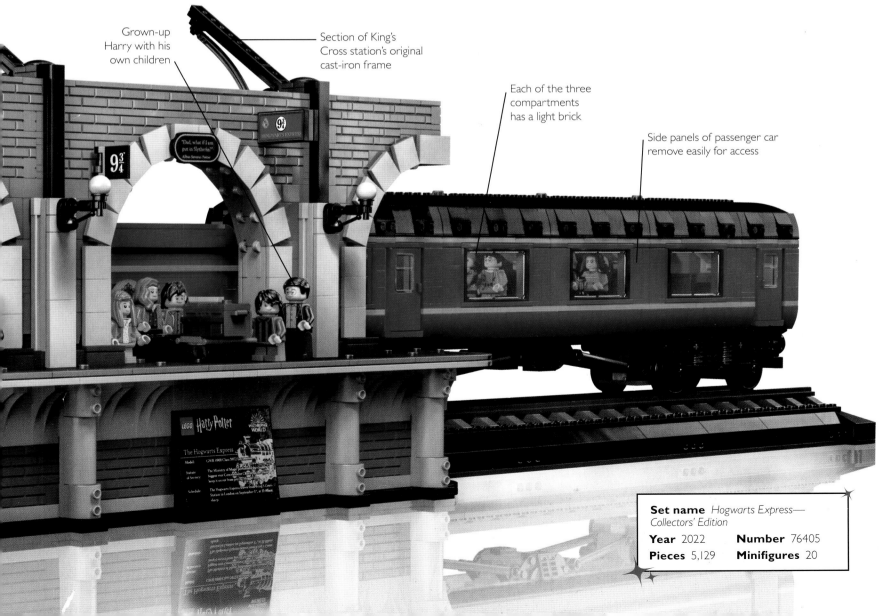

Grown-up Harry with his own children

Section of King's Cross station's original cast-iron frame

Each of the three compartments has a light brick

Side panels of passenger car remove easily for access

Set name *Hogwarts Express—Collectors' Edition*

Year 2022   **Number** 76405

Pieces 5,129   **Minifigures** 20

Head can rotate 360 degrees

Feathers attach to body with ball joints

Wing is a LEGO® hot-air balloon element

Set name
Hogwarts Icons—Collectors' Edition
Year 2021
Number 76391
Pieces 3,010
Minifigures 3

Acceptance letter from Hogwarts (you can even add your own name)

Golden Snitch's ball is a cube with a radar dish on each side

Potion tray has Hermione's initials and comes with four potion bottles

Page edges created by trapping stacks of upside-down panel pieces

Tom Riddle's diary

Harry's wand scaled for real human hands

Scarf can be built in any House colors

HOGWARTS

Dear _____,

We are pleased to inform you that you have been accepted at Hogwarts School of Witchcraft and Wizardry.

Yours Sincerely,

Prof. McGonagall

Professor McGonagall

HOGWARTS SCHOOL of WITCHCRAFT & WIZARDRY
Headmaster: Albus Dumbledore

INTRODUCTION

Within our world there exists another—a magical place that sits alongside our everyday lives, and you don't have to walk through a brick wall to find it. It's a place where one of the most popular toys combines with one of the biggest movie franchises to create something new and spectacular. It's the world of LEGO® Harry Potter™.

Delve into the pages of this book (thankfully with no monstrous, snapping pages) to discover how this spellbinding world has been recreated in LEGO sets since 2018.

Here, minifigures study magic, play Quidditch, and battle Dark forces. They live in incredible buildings, ride fantastical vehicles, and care for amazing creatures. Everything is brought to life, not with charms or transfiguration, but with the ingenious skills of LEGO designers and the versatility of LEGO bricks. See custom-made pieces, like the tiny Golden Snitch, and marvel at clever uses for classic

LEGO pieces: a LEGO frog in brown looks like a delicious chocolate treat and a ski pole turned upside down makes a perfect spire for Hogwarts' many towers.

In 2020, DK published LEGO *Harry Potter Magical Treasury*, but, without Hermione's Time-Turner, we couldn't see all the wonderful things to come. So this LEGO *Harry Potter Visual Dictionary* is an updated and expanded treasury. It shows recent innovations like lenticular backdrops for moving witch and wizard portraits and new elements like Pygmy Puffs. Plus, take a detailed glimpse into life at wizarding school with dedicated classrooms and common rooms, as well as the modular building system for the Hogwarts castle.

Get ready to enter into this wonderful, brick-built world of witches and wizards.

∨ DATA FILES

Throughout the book, you can find the key details of each LEGO set shown. A data file gives the official name, the year of its first release, its LEGO identification number, the number of LEGO pieces in it, and the number of minifigures it has.

Set name *Hogwarts Whomping Willow*	
Year 2018	**Number** 75953
Pieces 753	**Minifigures** 6

Ford Anglia crashed in tree

Hinged suitcases can be opened

Whomping Willow

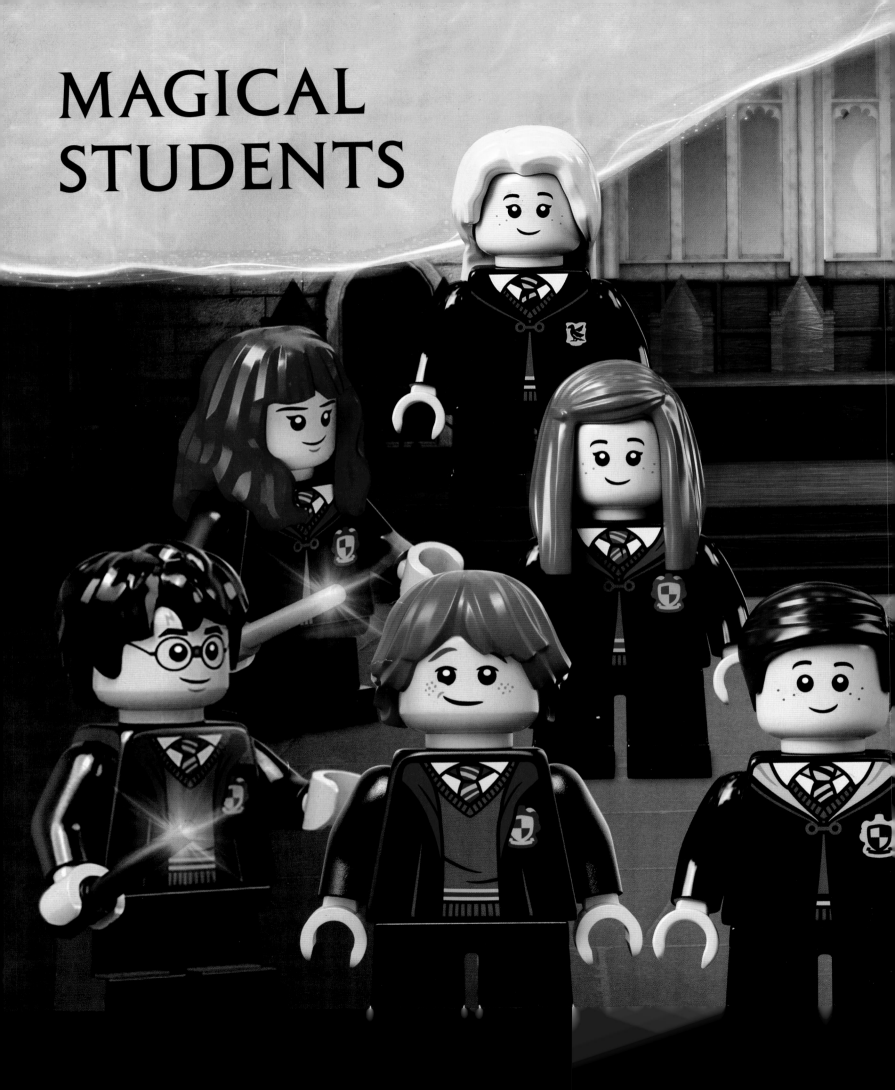

MAGICAL STUDENTS

HARRY POTTER

Harry Potter has had a very miserable life with his mean Aunt Petunia and Uncle Vernon and their bully of a son, Dudley. Harry believes that he is nothing special. But then, on his 11th birthday, everything changes. He discovers that not only is there a wizarding world full of magic, but that he himself is a wizard. In fact, he's a very famous one.

Belt stops oversized pants from falling down

▲ A NEW START

Harry has always had to wear his cousin Dudley's hand-me-downs —and they swamp his small frame. They are the only clothes he has until a kind half-giant called Hagrid takes Harry shopping for school supplies in Diagon Alley (set 75978).

James wears glasses like Harry

Scarf is its own LEGO® element

Lily's eye color is inherited by Harry

Baby Harry

Family photo from happier times

▲ JAMES AND LILY POTTER

Sadly, photos and magical memories are all Harry has of his parents. James and Lily Potter were killed by He Who Must Not Be Named when Harry was only one year old. But the Dursleys told Harry that they had died in a car crash.

Smart Gringotts uniform

Key to Harry's bank vault

Trolley cart rides the railroad

A SECRET FORTUNE

Harry needn't worry about how to pay for all his school supplies. At Gringotts Wizarding Bank, the goblin Griphook takes Harry on a hair-raising journey through the bank's winding tunnels to find his vault. It's full of wizard gold from his parents.

WAND SHOPPING

At Ollivanders wand shop, Harry learns that it's the wand who chooses the wizard or witch, not the other way around. After a few false starts, Harry finds the wand destined to be his. Its core is a phoenix feather, and it's linked to the wand that gave Harry his scar.

✴ OFF TO SCHOOL

Harry receives an acceptance letter from Hogwarts School of Witchcraft and Wizardry —even though he's never heard of it! He's all packed for his journey to school in this small set. It comes with all the supplies he needs, such as a pewter cauldron and a wand.

Set name	*Harry's Journey to Hogwarts*	
Year 2018	**Number** 30407	
Pieces 40	**Minifigures** 1	

Cauldron element with a metallic finish

This first-year Harry minifigure appears in four sets

Brand-new wand

LEGO® Technic holes look like wheels

HEDWIG

Hogwarts students are allowed to bring an owl, a cat, or a toad to school. Harry's snowy owl is named Hedwig and she came from Eeylops Owl Emporium. In the 2019 Advent Calendar (set 75964), she joins Harry with his trunk, a book, chocolate, and his letter of acceptance from Hogwarts.

SECOND YEAR

Harry sets off for his second year in a red shirt and gray pants. After missing the Hogwarts Express, he and Ron Weasley take Mr. Weasley's flying car.

Case packed for school

THIRD YEAR

In tan and blue, Harry's minifigure features in three sets based on his third-year adventures. But he needs to be careful—his life is increasingly dangerous.

Chocolate for eating on the Knight Bus

BRICK FACTS

All Harry's minifigures have his distinctive round glasses and lightning-bolt-shaped scar on his forehead. The length of Harry's leg piece varies depending on his age.

Longer hair sweeps across face

FOURTH YEAR

Harry's minifigure and his hair have grown! In 2018, the LEGO Group made a new leg piece. It's shorter than regular legs, but is hinged, unlike the shorter, unposeable leg piece.

Gray top has hood printed on the back

FIFTH YEAR

Now with full-size legs, Harry faces serious dangers. This minifigure encounters trouble in the Forbidden Forest and an attack on The Burrow.

Glasses smashed on the Hogwarts Express

SIXTH YEAR

Before Harry even steps inside Hogwarts castle for his sixth year, he's attacked by Draco Malfoy. It's not a good omen for what's to come.

PRIVET DRIVE

For as long as Harry can remember, home has always been his aunt and uncle's house, but it's not a happy place. Aunt Petunia and Uncle Vernon reluctantly took Harry in when his parents died, and they never made him feel welcome. This suburban house may not look very exciting, but it has helped keep Harry safe and hidden from Dark magical forces for many years.

∨ NUMBER 4

Mr. and Mrs. Dursley are very proud of their neat and tidy house in the Surrey town of Little Whinging. The LEGO model contains references from both the first and second movies—that's why Harry has two bedrooms. The main room has a shooting function that fires letters out of the fireplace.

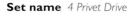

Set name	4 Privet Drive	
Year 2020	**Number** 75968	
Pieces 797	**Minifigures** 6	

Owl piece with outstretched wings

Barred window

Mr. Weasley's flying car "borrowed" by Ron

7990 TD

Ron pulls off Harry's bedroom window when he comes to collect him

BRICK FACTS

A unique LEGO sign for Privet Drive stands on two jumper plates. It also has a stud for an owl or a cat to sit on while they watch events in the street.

PRIVET DRIVE

Magical Hogwarts letters cannot get through the nailed-up letter box

UNDER THE STAIRS

For the first decade that Harry lives with the Dursleys, the only space he can call his own is a cramped area under the stairs. Even then, he still has to share it with a broom and shovel. The side wall of the LEGO house swings open to access his woeful sleeping space.

TO THE LETTER

On Harry's 11th birthday, he receives a mysterious letter delivered by owl, but Uncle Vernon won't let him read it. Number 4 Privet Drive is then magically flooded with letters. Can Harry keep hold of one long enough to read it, even though Vernon is determined to stop him?

Collared shirt under sweater

◄ DUDLEY DURSLEY

Harry and his cousin Dudley have nothing in common. Dudley's favorite hobby is making Harry's life miserable— just look at his smirk. "Dudders" is spoiled by his parents, and his minifigure's pants, hairstyle, and knitted sweater all make him look like a mini version of his dad, Vernon Dursley.

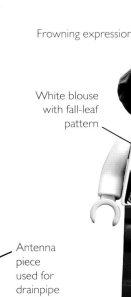

Frowning expression

White blouse with fall-leaf pattern

◄ AUNT PETUNIA

Harry's aunt could not be more different from her sister, Harry's mother, Lily Potter. Petunia has no magical ability—and cannot stand such nonsense. Her minifigure's sour expression sums up her attitude to anything unconventional, and particularly Harry. Petunia's appearance is always very prim and proper.

Antenna piece used for drainpipe

Well-tended flowerbeds

➤ UNCLE VERNON

Pompous Vernon Dursley is the head of his proudly Muggle family. He's used to everything being run his way and he gets very bad-tempered when it isn't. The other side of Vernon's dual-printed head has a slight smile, but it only appears when there is total peace and quiet.

Gray mustache quivers when Vernon is angry

Cloak has a shiny exterior and a printed pattern inside

HARRY AT HOGWARTS

Harry leaves behind his gloomy life with the Dursleys at Number 4 Privet Drive and finds his true home at Hogwarts School of Witchcraft and Wizardry. Harry soon makes friends, develops his magical abilities, and learns about wizard life. Unfortunately, there are challenges for Harry in the wizarding world too—and sometimes mortal danger.

FRIENDS FOREVER

Harry arrives for the school train, the Hogwarts Express, all alone, but it's not long before he starts making friends. He meets Ron Weasley, who becomes his best friend, and then Hermione Granger. Despite getting off to a rocky start, the three soon become a tight trio.

⋀ INVISIBILITY CLOAK

Harry receives a mysterious gift that used to belong to his father. It's a priceless cloak that makes him completely invisible. Harry and his friends find the cloak useful for moving around school after lights out. This Harry minifigure is sneaking around in his striped pajamas!

Snowflakes on Harry's personalized holiday sweater

⋖ AN HONORARY WEASLEY

Harry was treated poorly by his aunt and uncle, but he finds a loving family through his friend Ron. Ron's mother, Mrs. Weasley, treats Harry like one of her own children. She even knits him one of her famous woolly sweaters for his appearance in the LEGO® Harry Potter™ Advent Calendar (set 75964). Now he really looks like one of the family!

SORTING TIME!

When first years arrive at Hogwarts they all take part in the Sorting Ceremony. The Sorting Hat sits on their heads and magically determines which of the four school houses each will belong to. Harry is happy to join brave and noble Gryffindor—anything but Slytherin!

"Erised" is "desire" written backwards, as in a mirror

⋗ MIRROR OF ERISED

The Mirror of Erised doesn't reflect reality but the scene that your heart most desires—which can be a dangerous thing. For Harry, the brick-built mirror reflects the sight of himself with his parents, who were killed by Lord Voldemort when Harry was a baby. Other minifigures see different visions, thanks to four different sticker designs that come with the set.

Magical reflection

Set name	Hogwarts Great Hall	
Year	2018	Number 75954
Pieces	878	Minifigures 10

➤ QUIDDITCH STAR

Harry soon discovers Quidditch, a game played on broomsticks. It turns out that he's very good at it and he plays for his house, as Gryffindor's youngest Seeker in a century. His minifigure wears the team's scarlet-and-gold robes and bright-white pants—which won't stay white for long on a muddy pitch!

Warm, ribbed sweater underneath robes

Gryffindor crest

Leather flying gloves

Brick-built Triwizard Cup

Magical blue flames

◄ TRIWIZARD CHAMPION

The winner of the Triwizard Tournament wins eternal glory, but also money and this Triwizard Cup. To his shock, Harry is selected to take part in the contest. For one of the tournament's three tasks, he wears Gryffindor red but also a crest with all four houses. He is competing for the whole of Hogwarts, after all!

Acid pops printed on a minifigure head piece

The Marauder's Map

Short, smart haircut

Formal dress robes extend to full-sized legs

RULE BREAKER

Three of Harry's minifigures have this torso, but when paired with black trousers, he is on the Hogsmeade Village Visit (set 76388). But don't tell anyone—he sneaked out of school without permission!

MISCHIEF MAKER

Do you solemnly swear that you're up to no good? Then the Marauder's Map could help. Harry is gifted this magical map that reveals the location of everyone in Hogwarts—it's very useful for evading teachers!

SLUG CLUBBER

During Harry's sixth year he is invited to be part of Professor Slughorn's exclusive Slug Club—a collection of the professor's favorite students. At a Slug Club party in Hogwarts Astronomy Tower (set 75969), Harry wears his best black wizarding robes, but he is a reluctant guest because he doesn't like the special attention.

HERMIONE GRANGER

Crest with Gryffindor colors

The brightest witch of her age, fiercely intelligent Hermione Granger grew up in the Muggle world with dentist parents. She excels in her studies, but she's also good at using what she's learned in practical situations. Her knowledge and bravery have saved the day many times. Hermione is also a close and loyal friend to Harry and Ron—and not just because she keeps saving their lives!

Wizarding newspaper printed tile

MUGGLE WEAR

In Hogwarts Express (set 75955), Hermione is in casual Muggle clothes. She doesn't want to draw any attention at King's Cross Station.

⌃ MODEL STUDENT

Hermione is ready to learn in this Gryffindor school uniform with tie and crest. In Hogwarts Grand Staircase (set 40577), she comes with a pair of wands and two expressions—a knowing smirk and a nervous face for when she fears failure.

The Fat Lady portrait can be moved between arches

Set name
Harry Potter Advent Calendar

Year 2020

Number 75981

Pieces 335

Minifigures 6

Stair rail attaches with clip so it can move

◂ GRAND STAIRS

It takes some guts to walk down the Grand Staircase at Hogwarts—it moves! This magnificent stairwell is adorned with sticker portraits of Hogwart's finest wizards. The stair sides lift up and down and the whole staircase can rotate to connect to different rooms.

Round plates create ornate look

Set name
Hogwarts: Grand Staircase

Year 2022

Number 40577

Pieces 224

Minifigures 1

Wingardium leviosa!

◂ FROSTY FUN

Most students go home for the holidays, but Hermione prefers to perfect her bewitching skills. The 2020 LEGO Harry Potter Advent Calendar (set 75981) includes a frosty Christmas tree with a... star!

⌄ TOP OF THE CLASS

In LEGO Harry Potter Series 1 (71022), Hermione's minifigure has a more grown-up face print and a slender hairstyle with no bangs. She wears a long, maroon-lined robe and is accompanied by her cat, Crookshanks.

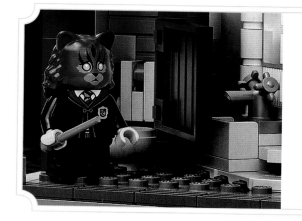

MAGICAL MIX-UP

Hermione is excellent at potions and can master complex concoctions like Polyjuice Potion. But potion skills don't help when the hair Hermione stole to impersonate Millicent Bulstrode actually came from a cat. Hermione's minifigure is half-Slytherin witch and half-cat!

This LEGO cat mold is used in this color only for Crookshanks

Time-Turner worn around neck

TIME TRAVELER

In Hagrid's Hut: Buckbeak's Rescue (set 75947), Hermione uses a Time-Turner so that she can repeat the day to take more classes.

Handheld Time-Turner

Bandage on arm

WORSE FOR WEAR

Hermione has a bandaged hand and muddy jacket in Hogwarts: Hospital Wing (76398), after scrambling under the Whomping Willow.

Sleek, straight hair

SERIOUS STUFF

Sixth-year Hermione practices Defense Against the Dark Arts for Dumbledore's Army in Hogwarts: Room of Requirement (set 75966).

BRICK FACTS

Patronuses are defensive charms that take the form of a shimmering animal. Hermione's is an otter. Its semi-solid shape is captured in a transparent blue glittery LEGO piece.

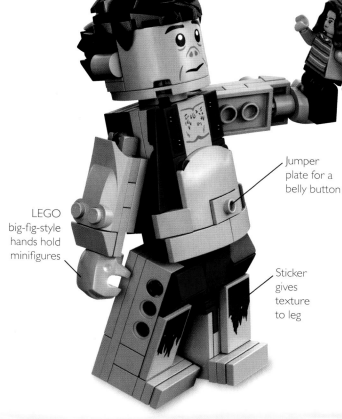

LEGO big-fig-style hands hold minifigures

Jumper plate for a belly button

Sticker gives texture to leg

Bicycle bell

Set name	*Forbidden Forest: Umbridge's Encounter*	
Year 2020		**Number** 75967
Pieces 253		**Minifigures** 3

◁ A FIRM HAND

Hermione is not afraid to tell giant Grawp to put her down when she meets him in the Forbidden Forest (set 75967). He takes a shine to Hermione and gives her a trinket as a token of his affection—bicycle handle bars with a bell that they use to communicate with each other.

17

Bald patch printed on Scabbers' head

Untidy uniform

RON WEASLEY

Ron comes from a big, boisterous family. He meets Harry at King's Cross station on the first day of school and they become close friends. Sometimes Ron feels second best compared to his older brothers or his famous friend, but he proves himself to be a worthy Gryffindor: courageous, brave, and determined. These qualities help him on many adventures.

Red hair is a Weasley family trait

Freckles

Check jacket

⋀ RAT KEEPER

Ron's pet rat, Scabbers, joins him at Hogwarts and in the first LEGO Harry Potter series of minifigures (71022). Ron looks a little older now he is in his third year. He also has a unique torso—that's because no one else has such a bedraggled uniform.

➤ BRAVE ADVENTURER

Ron follows in his five older brothers' footsteps when he sets off for school on his short LEGO legs in Hogwarts Express (set 75955). The same brave minifigure carries a lantern to light his way when he ventures into the Forbidden Forest in Aragog's Lair (set 75950).

Goblets of pumpkin juice

Long refectory benches for each house

⋀ EVERY DAY IS A FEAST

Mealtimes at Hogwarts are a highlight of Ron's day. His stomach thinks about food a lot and he enjoys all the sumptuous dishes that the Hogwarts kitchens produce and deliver to the tables like magic!

Set name
Harry Potter Advent Calendar
Year 2020
Number 75981
Pieces 335
Minifigures 6

DOGGED DETERMINATION

Ron can be quite scared of things—things like fierce three-headed dogs with three sets of snarling teeth. (Only Hagrid would call such a beast "Fluffy!") But Ron doesn't let his fear hold him back. He and his friends are set on saving the mysterious Sorcerer's Stone so he conquers his terror and leaps.

CHESS MASTER

Ron loves Wizard Chess. All his practice pays off when he faces the ultimate challenge in a chess game of life or death. As Dumbledore says, it's "the best-played game of chess that Hogwarts has seen these many years."

Ron directs his friends across the board

Life-sized chess board

Chess pieces get defeated for good

Set name
Hogwarts Wizard's Chess
Year 2021
Number 76392
Pieces 876
Minifigures 4

BRICK FACTS

Two double-sided panels come with the Mirror of Erised. The reflections can be swapped depending on who looks in the mirror. Ron sees himself as Head Boy and Quidditch Captain.

House Cup

Bare, gnarly branches hold car in place

Secret entrance to a tunnel beneath the tree

Set name *Hogwarts Whomping Willow*
Year 2018   **Number** 75953
Pieces 753   **Minifigures** 6

◄ RUNAWAY RON

Having missed the Hogwarts Express in their second year, Ron and Harry set off for school in Mr. Weasley's flying car. The boys make it to Hogwarts in the vehicle, but they crash-land in the Whomping Willow. They're stuck there until the tree violently shakes them out.

WON WON

Now in his sixth year at Hogwarts, Ron has full-sized minifigure legs. In Hogwarts Astronomy Tower (set 75969), he explores the castle with fellow Gryffindor Lavender Brown. The pair exchange presents, and romance blossoms between Lavender and her "Won Won."

Temporary walking cane

"R" for "Ron"

Plaster cast

Hair is long in the fourth year

Frilly dress robes

HOLIDAY SWEATER

Every Christmas Ron gets a personalized sweater from his mother. He finds them embarrassing, but they are knitted with love and are affordable presents.

ONE-LEGGED RON

Ron is surprisingly cheerful given he's in Hogwarts Hospital Wing (set 76398) with a broken leg. A strange black dog dragged him down into the Whomping Willow.

BEHIND THE TIMES

Poor Ron does not enjoy the Yule Ball. Hermione is going with Viktor Krum and, to make matters worse, Ron has to wear old-fashioned robes that his mother sent. In Ron's own words, they make him look like his Great-Aunt Tessie!

THE BURROW

The Weasleys don't have the latest fashions and gadgets, but they do have a cozy place to live. The wonky but much-loved Burrow is a welcome second home for Harry. Filled with chatter, laughter, and wizarding wonders, it couldn't be more different from Privet Drive. But Harry puts it at risk when he stays, drawing the fire of some sinister witches and wizards.

Set name *Attack on the Burrow*
Year 2020 **Number** 75980
Pieces 1,047 **Minifigures** 8

◂ HODGEPODGE HOUSE

Located near the Devon village of Ottery St. Catchpole, The Burrow looks like a physical impossibility. With its wobbly frame, it looks like it's held up by magic! The house grew as the family did, with extra rooms piled on the top. This LEGO model captures its higgledy-piggledy style over four slanting floors.

RON'S BEDROOM

During the school breaks, Ron writes letters for Pigwidgeon to carry to Harry—when Harry isn't staying in The Burrow, that is! Ron has decorated his room with a Chudley Cannons poster and his bedding is the same bright orange as the Quidditch team's robes.

FLOO IN THE FIRE

The Burrow is connected to the Floo Network—a transport grid along which people can be transported using magic powder. Entrances to the network are fireplaces and this LEGO one has a mechanism to change the flames from orange to green as the floo powder burns.

Roof terrace for minifigures

Wooden planks show regular repairs

Roof patched up in different shades

Wooden frame is a remnant of the original Tudor dwelling

Hinged bricks make the upper floors tip at a crooked angle

Ancient stained-glass window

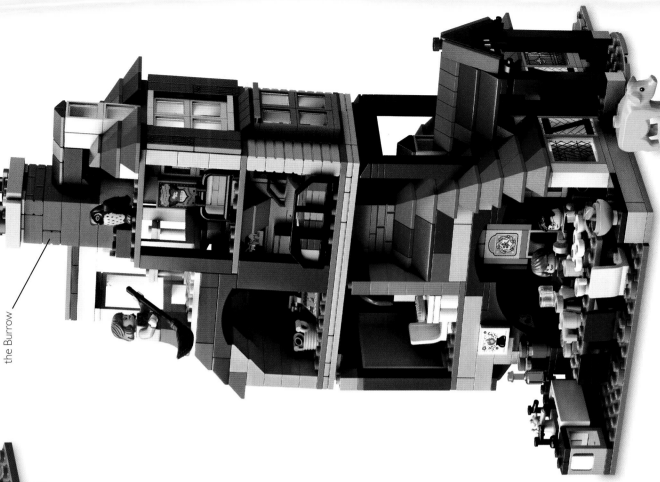

Rear view of the Burrow

HEART OF THE HOME

The kitchen, where Molly Weasley prepares enormous meals with the help of magic, fills most of the ground floor. In pride of place is a grandfather-style clock. Instead of the time, the clock face indicates the location of each member of the family—or if they're in mortal danger.

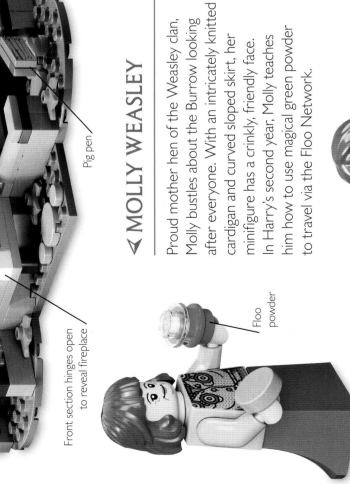

Pig pen

Front section hinges open to reveal fireplace

MOLLY WEASLEY

Proud mother hen of the Weasley clan, Molly bustles about the Burrow looking after everyone. With an intricately knitted cardigan and curved sloped skirt, her minifigure has a crinkly, friendly face. In Harry's second year, Molly teaches him how to use magical green powder to travel via the Floo Network.

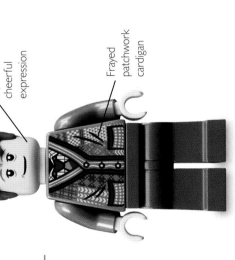

Open and cheerful expression

Frayed patchwork cardigan

ARTHUR WEASLEY

A warm, kind wizard, Arthur Weasley works for the Misuse of Muggle Artifacts Office at the Ministry of Magic. He's fascinated by all things Muggle. Much of the Burrow's clutter is made up of items he's brought home to figure out how they work, and he marvels at their magic-free technology.

Floo powder

PERCY WEASLEY

Percy—the third-oldest brother—grows up in the Burrow, but he's looking forward to leaving home as soon as he can. He has his sights set on an influential job at the Ministry of Magic. In the meantime, he proudly wears his hard-earned Head Boy school badge. His minifigure was an exclusive release with DK's book LEGO *Harry Potter: A Spellbinding Guide to Hogwarts Houses*.

Wand is ready to stop rule breakers

LEGO hair piece was first designed for Ginny

GINNY WEASLEY

The youngest of the Weasley brood of seven children, Ginny is the only daughter. She finally gets to follow all her brothers to Hogwarts at the beginning of Harry and Ron's second year. The Sorting Hat recognizes her grit and strength and, like everyone in her family, she becomes part of Gryffindor. Ginny is a keen Quidditch player and represents her house on the pitch.

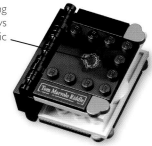

Basilisk fang damage destroys the diary's magic

BROUGHT TO BOOK

Ginny falls foul of evil plots during her first year. She pours her heart into Tom Riddle's diary, but the Dark magical object puts her in great danger.

⋀ CHARMED STUDENT

A short minifigure with nonposeable legs, Ginny looks very young when she starts at Hogwarts. As she grows, her minifigures get longer legs, evolving hair styles, and older face prints, but they always have her trademark red locks.

HOME, SWEET HOME

Ginny enjoys a peaceful cup of tea in her bedroom at the busy, crowded Burrow. Her green bedding celebrates her favorite Quidditch team, the Holyhead Harpies, and she has a Weird Sisters band poster on her wall.

AFTER A SPELL

Long after Ginny studies at Hogwarts, it's the next generation's turn. On September 1, she arrives at King's Cross station with her husband—a certain Harry Potter—and their children: Lily Luna, James Sirius, and Albus Severus. Albus is about to take his first journey on the Hogwarts Express.

Profiterole desert

BRICK FACTS

Delightful balls of fluff, Pygmy Puff pets are sold at Weasleys' Wizard Wheezes. Almost spherical, the creature's LEGO piece can be held by a minifigure.

⋖ RISING STAR

Bright, quick, and spirited, Ginny catches the attention of Professor Slughorn. He's always on the lookout for talent, and her spot on the Quidditch team earns her an invite to Slughorn's fancy Slug Club dinner.

Prominent front teeth

Baby Mandrake root

NEVILLE LONGBOTTOM

Neville is friends with Harry, Ron, and Hermione and is with them in Gryffindor House. When he's not at school, he's raised by his overbearing grandmother. She can be quick to criticize the shy boy, but he makes her very proud in the end, and he lives up to his family's legacy of standing up against Dark magical forces.

Slanted tile props book open

BOOKED!

Despite being a natural at Herbology, Neville struggles in many lessons. He's terrorized by the ferocious *Monster Book of Monsters*—if only he knew to stroke its spine to subdue it!

⬆ GREEN FINGERS

Neville needn't look so concerned. He's a whizz at Herbology so he isn't going to be caught out when the Mandrake he is repotting begins its ear-piercing scream. The earmuffs built into Neville's hair piece block the noise, while an overcoat protects his uniform from soil.

FIGHT OR FLIGHT

Draco Malfoy takes every opportunity to taunt anyone he regards as inferior to him—and that definitely includes Neville. Draco has snatched Neville's new Remembrall sent by his grandmother and is flying off with it. Poor old Neville isn't a confident flier and struggles to keep up.

BRICK FACTS

This transparent minifigure head with unique printing is a Remembrall. Its red bloom means that Neville has forgotten something—but he can't recall what!

Sword of Gryffindor has a hilt inset with rubies

TRUE GRYFFINDOR

Although he may seem timid, Neville has nerves of steel and determination to match. When Hogwarts is under threat, he bravely fulfils a special task with the Sword of Gryffindor.

➢ A WAITING GAME

Some students like Hermione are singled out by Professor Slughorn to be his special guests. Others, like Neville, are considered by Slughorn to make good waiters. Good-natured Neville doesn't mind serving drinks and canapés to his friends.

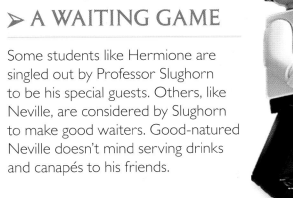

Tray clips into minifigure's hand

Formal waiting uniform

PLATFORM 9¾

All aboard the Hogwarts Express! Every September 1 this gleaming steam train leaves London King's Cross station to take students to Hogwarts for the new school year. This set includes a section of the station with platforms 9, 10, the mysterious platform 9¾, and the 2018 LEGO version of the famous scarlet locomotive.

LUGGAGE CAR

Between the train's engine and the passenger carriage is a linked coal car. The hinged top plate can be lifted up, revealing lots of space for students' luggage underneath—or a place for a minifigure to hide from the terrifying Dementor that comes with the set.

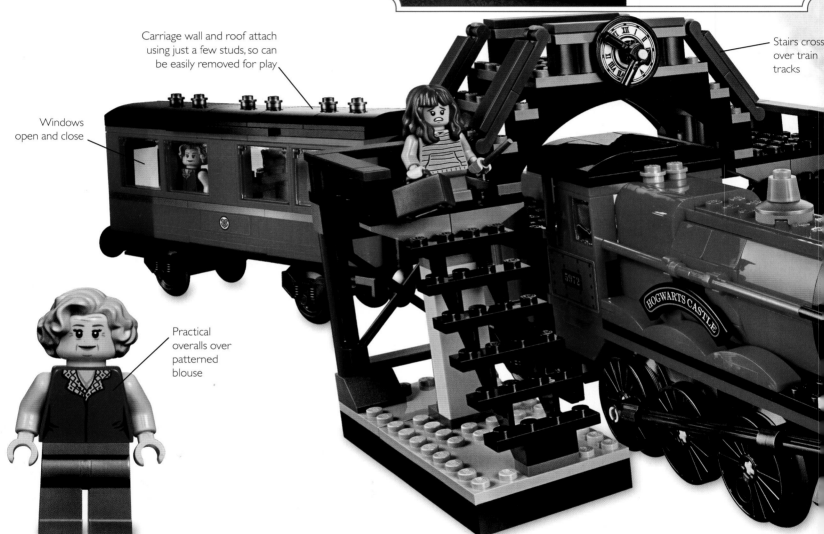

Carriage wall and roof attach using just a few studs, so can be easily removed for play

Windows open and close

Stairs cross over train tracks

Practical overalls over patterned blouse

A TROLLEY WITCH

This kind, elderly witch has been selling food and drink on the Hogwarts Express for many years. Generations of students have looked forward to the rattle of her snack trolley coming along the carriage. Her minifigure has wrinkles on her face and smartly coiffed hair.

HONEYDUKES EXPRESS

The Hogwarts Express gets students to school, but it's the Honeydukes Express snack trolley that fills their stomachs and satisfies their sweet tooth. It's stocked with candy, ice-cream, drinks, and even a Chocolate Frog—just make sure it doesn't jump out of the open window!

ⅴ PLATFORM 9¾

Ask a Muggle for directions to Platform 9¾ and they'll think you're trying to be funny. This secret platform is invisible to them. To Muggles, its entrance just looks like a solid brick wall located between the ordinary platforms 9 and 10. But behind it is where you'll find the Hogwarts Express. This special LEGO train has three sections: the distinctive red locomotive, a luggage or coal car, and a passenger carriage with seats for four minifigures.

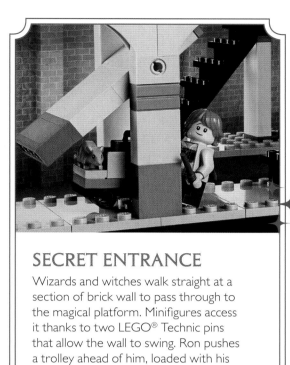

SECRET ENTRANCE

Wizards and witches walk straight at a section of brick wall to pass through to the magical platform. Minifigures access it thanks to two LEGO® Technic pins that allow the wall to swing. Ron pushes a trolley ahead of him, loaded with his luggage and pet rat, Scabbers.

Solid wall swings up so Ron can pass through

Wanted poster shows Sirius Black

Large printed radar dish fronts the 2018 version of the train

BRICK FACTS

A specially printed 4x4 radar dish sits at the front of the 2018 train. It's printed with "5972" because the design of the train is based on the Great Western Railway 5972 Olton Hall steam train.

Set name	*Hogwarts Express*
Year 2018	**Number** 75955
Pieces 801	**Minifigures** 5

HOGSMEADE STATION

Alight here for Hogwarts! This way please! Every September 1 at 11am, the magical Hogwarts Express leaves London to carry young witches and wizards to Hogsmeade village station for the new school year at Hogwarts. Hagrid greets the students on the platform and leads them to the school. This 2023 LEGO set includes the little station with its ticket office and restroom, as well as the train, track, and signpost.

STATION ROOMS

Inside the station there is a cozy ticket office with a fireplace and a London-to-Hogsmeade journey map on the wall. Harry Potter has his precious Hogwarts Express ticket and is clasping it, ready to go. The trip to Hogwarts is long, so young wizards and witches are relieved to know that there is also a restroom at the station.

OWL POST

Hogsmeade Station has its own Owl Post room where eager owls wait to pick up urgent letters and parcels. Owl Post is faster than Muggles' mail and is a common way for wizards to communicate with each other. Harry Potter's snowy white owl is named Hedwig.

Green tiles are moss

Bright-red bricks support station sign

Macaroni-shaped name plate fronts the 2023 LEGO train

Harry Potter's family photo album

Set name *Hogwarts Express Train Set with Hogsmeade Station*
Year 2023   **Number** 76423
Pieces 1,074   **Minifigures** 8

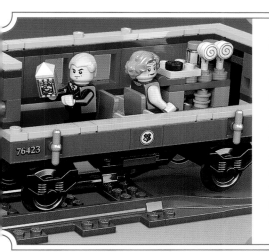

SUPER SNACKS

It might be a tight squeeze when all the students are on board the train, but there's always room for the refreshments cart. The Trolley Witch has a delicious stock of candy, ice cream, and even Chocolate Frogs. Maybe they're a little tastier than the Every Flavor Bean that Draco Malfoy is about to eat!

BRICK FACTS

Bertie Bott's Every Flavor Beans come in a huge variety of flavors—from peppermint to ketchup and even earwax. You don't know what you've got until you taste it!

Large, pointed lid closes the bean jar

▽ HOGWARTS EXPRESS

All aboard! The famous Hogwarts Express is pulled by a crimson locomotive with a shiny name plate, a coal car, two passenger carriages, each with room for four minifigures, and a friendly train conductor. The locomotive's front buffer beam can be turned to let the train travel off the track.

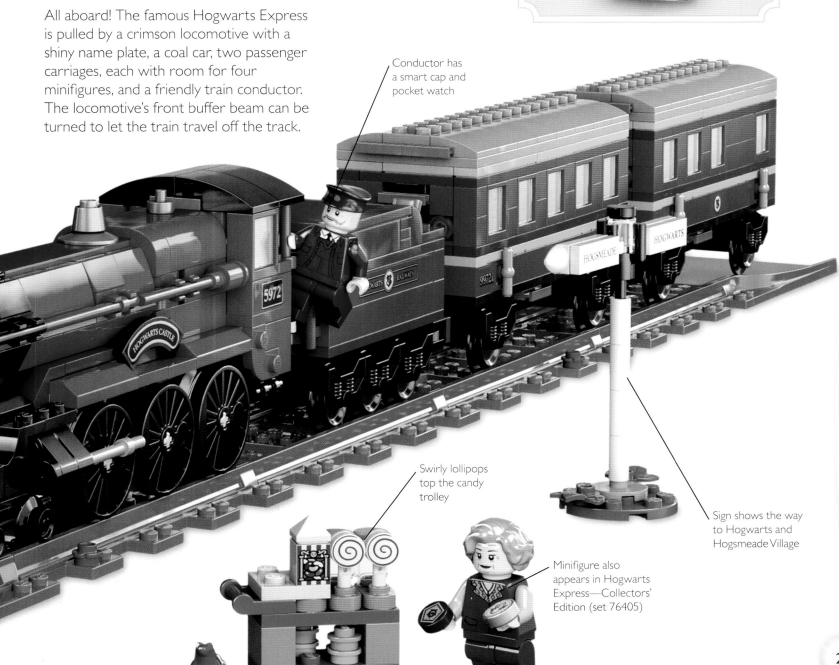

Conductor has a smart cap and pocket watch

Swirly lollipops top the candy trolley

Sign shows the way to Hogwarts and Hogsmeade Village

Minifigure also appears in Hogwarts Express—Collectors' Edition (set 76405)

Alternative face print wears Spectrespecs

HOGWARTS STUDENTS

Harry, Ron, and Hermione aren't the only young wizards and witches at Hogwarts. During the course of his studies, Harry finds a number of friends—and rivals—among his fellow students. Many of these classmates can be found in the LEGO Harry Potter Series 1 and 2 and they come with their own special accessories.

◢ LUNA LOVEGOOD

Nothing sums up quirky Luna better than her eccentric outfits. She claims her colorful Spectrespecs reveal Wrackspurts—invisible creatures that cause brain fog. She's a fan of her father's newspaper, *The Quibbler*, even though most say it's full of nonsense.

➤ DRACO MALFOY

It's no surprise that the Sorting Hat placed Draco in Slytherin—he's ruthless and focused on what he wants. Draco is a bully who thinks he's better than everyone else because of his elitist family and his wealth.

Hair always worn swept back

Slytherin tie

Skirt folds all the way around legs

Owl can clip onto minifigure hand

◢ CHO CHANG

Cho Chang was the first minifigure to appear wearing the Ravenclaw House tie. Here her uniform, like Luna Lovegood's minifigure, also includes a special LEGO skirt made from a type of fabric that is similar to previous minifigures' capes. The skirt is held in place between her torso and leg pieces.

LIKE FATHER, LIKE SON

Look no further to see where Draco gets his cruel streak and sense of superiority. His father, Lucius Malfoy, is used to getting his own way and will threaten anyone who isn't doing what he wants—even his own son.

➤ SUSAN BONES

This cheery minifigure is one of Harry's Hufflepuff classmates, Susan Bones. She was the first minifigure to wear the yellow-and-black Hufflepuff tie. Her smiling face turns around to reveal a worried one: well, she is in Hogwarts Great Hall (set 75954) when the Chamber of Secrets opens!

Hufflepuff tie

Short, nonposeable legs

Freckles on cheeks

◄ SEAMUS FINNIGAN

Gryffindor Seamus looks cheerful here, but the other side of his freckled face shows alarm. He appears in Hogwarts Whomping Willow (set 75953), where Harry and Ron come smashing into the school grounds in a flying blue car. It's hard to say what's more terrifying—a crashing car or the thrashing branches of the ferocious magical tree.

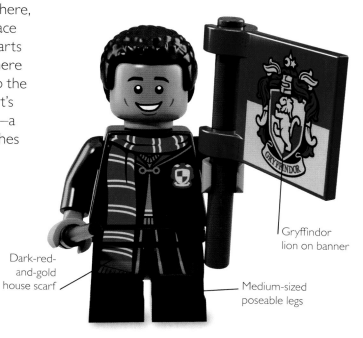

Gryffindor lion on banner

Dark-red-and-gold house scarf

Medium-sized poseable legs

➤ LAVENDER BROWN

A fellow Gryffindor in Harry's year, Lavender Brown wears her heart on her sleeve—and printed all over her torso. She is brave and bold, as well as having a softer side, too.

Fitted tops layered up under chunky necklace

⩘ DEAN THOMAS

All wrapped up against the cold, Dean Thomas is ready to go out and cheer for Gryffindor on the Quidditch pitch. Dean is a big fan of Quidditch, but his real love is soccer played by Muggles. He brightens up life at Hogwarts with his straight-talking and practical attitude.

BRICK FACTS

During his sixth year at Hogwarts, several girls had crushes on Harry and talked about using a love potion on him, including Romilda Vane who actually tried one.

Distinctive freckles

Gray top is similar to Hogwarts uniforms

➤ ROMILDA VANE

Romilda Vane and Lavender are friends and fellow Gryffindors who go shopping together in Diagon Alley: Weasleys' Wizard Wheezes (set 76422). This is Romilda's first minifigure, from 2023.

QUIDDITCH

The roar of the crowd, the flash of broomsticks, the clash of winners and losers, the risk of injury... they all mean one thing: a Hogwarts Quidditch match! The favorite sport of wizards and witches, Quidditch is a ball game played on broomsticks, and Harry is a natural. Every match is an event that the whole school comes to watch.

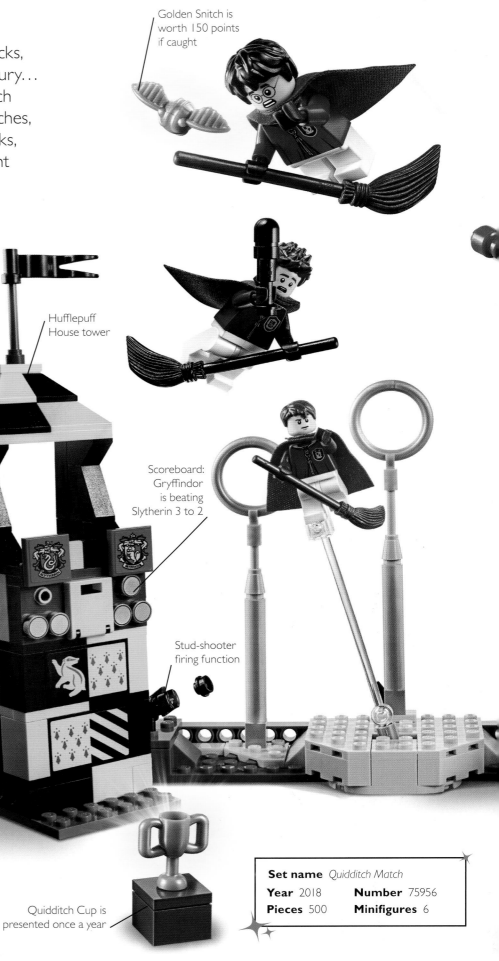

Golden Snitch is worth 150 points if caught

Slytherin spectator tower

Hufflepuff House tower

Scoreboard: Gryffindor is beating Slytherin 3 to 2

Magical fire created by Hermione to distract Snape

Stud-shooter firing function

Each tower is built using house colors

Quidditch Cup is presented once a year

Set name *Quidditch Match*
Year 2018   **Number** 75956
Pieces 500   **Minifigures** 6

▼ GAME ON!

Slytherin Chaser Marcus Flint shoots the Quaffle. Can Gryffindor's Keeper, Oliver Wood, keep him from scoring a goal? Meanwhile, Beater Lucian Bole wants to put Harry off his game with a Bludger, or even with his bat. But Harry is already in enough trouble. His broom is behaving very oddly!

ON THE BALL

Quidditch is a game of four balls: the red Quaffle, the Golden Snitch, and two violent Bludgers. This set, however, comes with extra Bludgers that can be fired at minifigures from a real LEGO stud-shooter.

Red flag tops Gryffindor tower

Ravenclaw supporters' tower

Chest for storing all three types of ball

Hinged door through which players enter the pitch

BRICK FACTS

LEGO stud-shooters have been seen on vehicles and even as minifigure-held weapons, but this is the first time one has been mounted on a broomstick.

HE SHOOTS... HE SCORES!

For 10 points, the Quaffle must be thrown through one of three hooped goalposts. Oliver Wood's minifigure perches on a moving pole to defend all three hoops. Marcus Flint's broom features a shooting function to launch the Quaffle at the goals.

ROARING SUPPORT

Despite being a proud Ravenclaw, Luna Lovegood supports her Gryffindor friends with elaborate headwear shaped like their house animal—a brave lion!

31

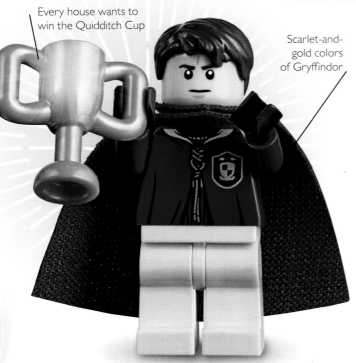

Every house wants to win the Quidditch Cup

Scarlet-and-gold colors of Gryffindor

QUIDDITCH PLAYERS

All first-year students take flying lessons, but only a few make it onto a house Quidditch team. Seven players from each house are selected to compete for the Quidditch Cup and glory for their team. These talented players are all speedy on a broom, nimble at dodging Bludgers, and eagle-eyed.

Slicked-back blond hair

Shorter cape than Slytherin teammates

Broom handle fits a minifigure hand

⌃ OLIVER WOOD

As Gryffindor Captain and Keeper, it's Oliver Wood's job to both lead the team and guard the goal hoops to prevent the other team from scoring goals with the Quaffle. His minifigure has a determined expression and he pushes his players—particularly against Slytherin.

2023 ribbed Quidditch torso

➤ ANGELINA JOHNSON

When Oliver Wood leaves school, he passes the baton of Gryffindor Captain to Angelina Johnson. As a fiercely dedicated player, it's fitting that her first LEGO minifigure is dressed ready for Quidditch.

⌃ DRACO MALFOY

Draco Malfoy and Harry Potter don't get along at the best of times, but their rivalry really comes out on the Quidditch pitch. Draco is the Slytherin Seeker, so the two boys are in competition to see who will catch the Golden Snitch first. With his scowling face, Draco looks determined to beat Harry.

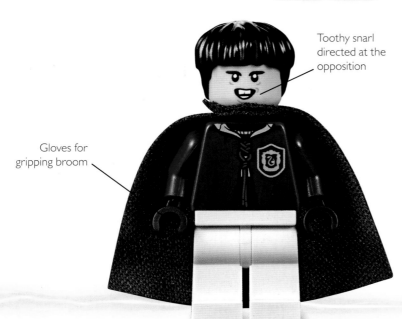

Toothy snarl directed at the opposition

Gloves for gripping broom

◄ MARCUS FLINT

The Slytherin Quidditch Captain, Marcus Flint is the direct rival of Oliver Wood. Flint drives his team hard as well—but doesn't always make them play by the rules. Until Harry Potter joined the game, the Slytherin team was the reigning champion—and that's not a title that they'll give up easily.

◀ LUCIAN BOLE

Armed with a hefty bat in Quidditch Match (set 75956), Lucian Bole is one of Slytherin's two Beaters. His role is to use the bat to hit the Bludgers away from his teammates and towards the other team. But unfair Lucian has been known to use his bat directly on rival players.

Wind-ruffled hair piece shared with Seamus Finnigan

Green-and-~~er~~ Slytherin robes

Nimbus 2001 from Draco's father

Spiky gray hair

Brass whistle for refereeing

Black teacher's robes

➤ CEDRIC DIGGORY

As well as being the Captain of the , Hufflepuff team, Cedric plays as Seeker. Sociable and easy-going, he's a popular player on the pitch, and he wears a ribbed Quidditch sweater in Hufflepuff House Banner (set 76412.)

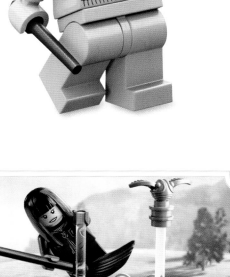

⋏ MADAM HOOCH

Rolanda Hooch is Hogwarts' strict flying instructor and Quidditch referee. She's an expert on the subject of broomsticks and her minifigure comes with a brown one. She wears yellow-tinted flying goggles, and the other side of her dual head shows a more stern expression, without goggles.

Diadem of Ravenclaw

⋎ DRESSING FOR SUCCESS

In 2023, the LEGO Group introduced new Quidditch robes with molded capes instead of fabric ones. Harry, Cho, Cedric, and Draco each represent their houses in Quidditch Trunk (set 76416).

GRYFFINDOR

RAVENCLAW

⋏ CHO CHANG

~~C~~ho Chang is Ravenclaw's Seeker ~~s~~o, like Harry, Draco, and Cedric, ~~sh~~e has to find the Golden Snitch ~~b~~efore the other team's Seeker ~~do~~es. In 2023, minifigures got a ~~se~~cond Quidditch outfit—a ~~ri~~bbed sweater rather than ~~stri~~ped robes with tie fastenings, ~~an~~d tan pants instead of white.

QUIDDITCH PRACTICE

Cho Chang comes in the Quidditch Practice (set 30651) polybag. She uses the spinning center of the microscale pitch to practice catching the Golden Snitch. Cho wears the torso from the mannequin in Diagon Alley (set 75978), but she is the only minifigure to have Quidditch legs in her house color.

HUFFLEPUFF

SLYTHERIN

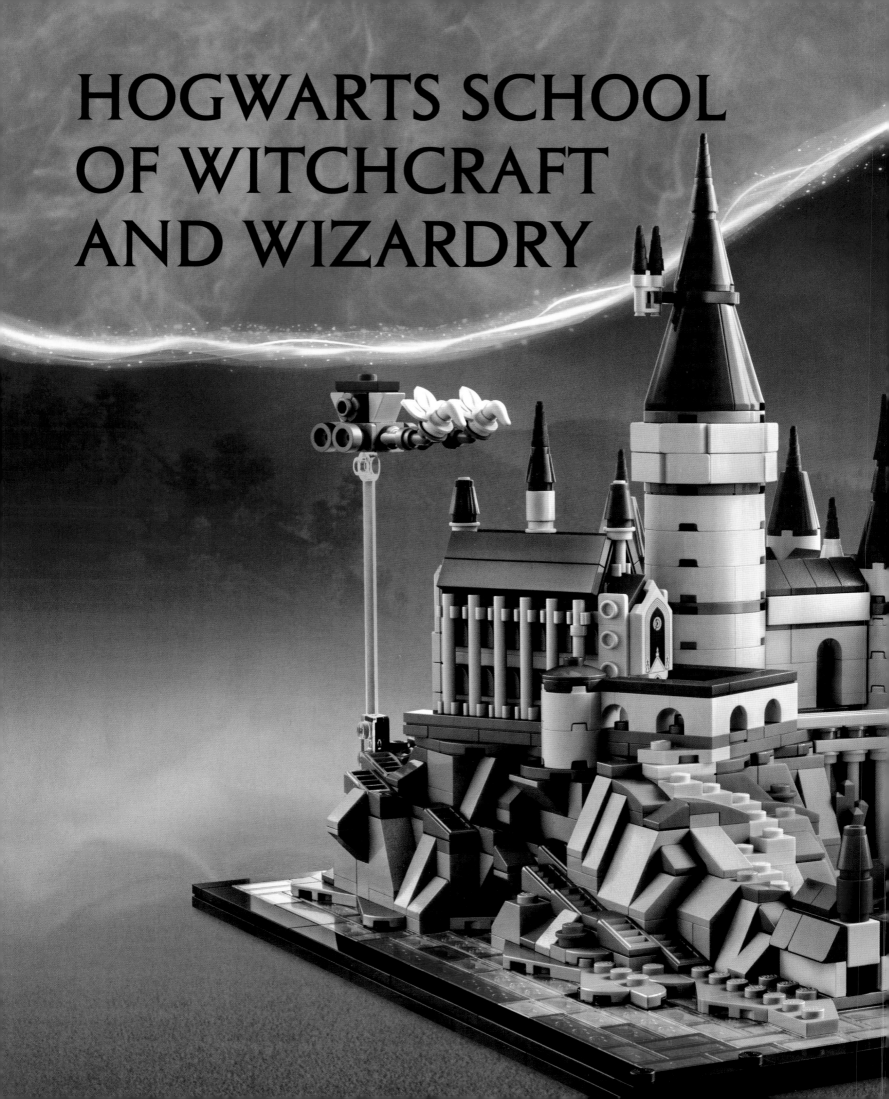

HOGWARTS SCHOOL OF WITCHCRAFT AND WIZARDRY

Hogwarts™ Castle

HOGWARTS CASTLE

Welcome to Hogwarts School of Witchcraft and Wizardry—and congratulations on finding it. This ancient castle of imposing towers and conical spires perches atop a remote mountain. Powerful magic prevents its location in the Scottish Highlands being plotted on a map. Although the castle is more than 1,000 years old, it is as strong as ever, sturdily built in stone and held together by enchantments.

➤ MICROSCALE CASTLE

This is the most extensive LEGO® set of Hogwarts ever made. Such is the castle's size that even in microscale—smaller proportions than the usual minifigure scale—this model uses more than 6,000 pieces and is 29½ in (75 cm) wide. The set includes minifigures of the four Hogwarts founders, who can be displayed on a separate stand.

Set name *Hogwarts Castle*	
Year 2018	**Number** 71043
Pieces 6,020	**Minifigures** 4 (plus 27 microfigures)

Escaped Hungarian Horntail dragon clir to roof tiles

Back of a gray tooth piece makes a gable window

Brick-built cladding cove round panels

Transparent bricks for stained-glass windows

Boathouse

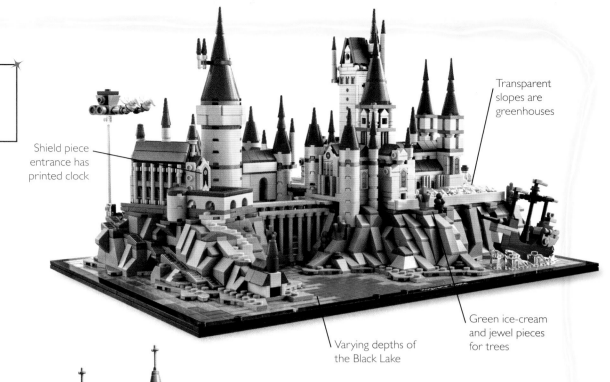

Set name *Hogwarts Castle and Grounds*

Year 2023   **Number** 76419

Pieces 2,660   **Minifigures** 1

▶ HOGWARTS REVISITED

In 2023, a second microscale model of Hogwarts Castle was created. Details like the Durmstrang Ship and the Beauxbatons Carriage retell moments from the Triwizard Tournament in Harry's fourth year. The large castle comes with a golden minifigure of the never-before-seen architect of Hogwarts.

Shield piece entrance has printed clock

Transparent slopes are greenhouses

Green ice-cream and jewel pieces for trees

Varying depths of the Black Lake

Turrets of different sizes top stone towers

Gray beard

Bald patch

Slytherin house tie

PROFESSOR DUMBLEDORE

ARGUS FILCH

SLYTHERIN STUDENT

⋏ MICROFIGURES

This huge set is inhabited by 27 tiny microscale figures, including staff, students from each house, and even five scary Dementors! The mold for the figures was first used to make trophies for minifigures to hold. Its base fits onto a single stud.

Microfigures walk over viaduct

Evergreen trees are upside-down flower stems stacked on a pole

THE GREAT HALL

The imposing size of Hogwarts castle and its peculiar, magical ways can be a little overwhelming for students. New students are taken immediately to the Great Hall to be sorted into one of the four Hogwarts houses. For Harry, who never felt like he belonged with the Dursleys, Hogwarts is the best place he's ever known and it soon feels like home—despite the floating candles and moving staircases!

BRICK FACTS

This 1x1 brick with a scroll has added grandeur to LEGO sets since 2015. Perfect for Hogwarts' ornate architecture, it features in pale yellow for stone and in brown for wood.

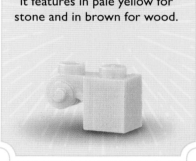

➤ A HOME FROM HOME

The Great Hall set includes a dining room with four long tables for students and a raised High Table for teachers. At one end of the Hall is a four-story tower with a Potions classroom, a room with treasure, and an attic in the turret. The set draws inspiration from Harry's adventures in his first two years at Hogwarts.

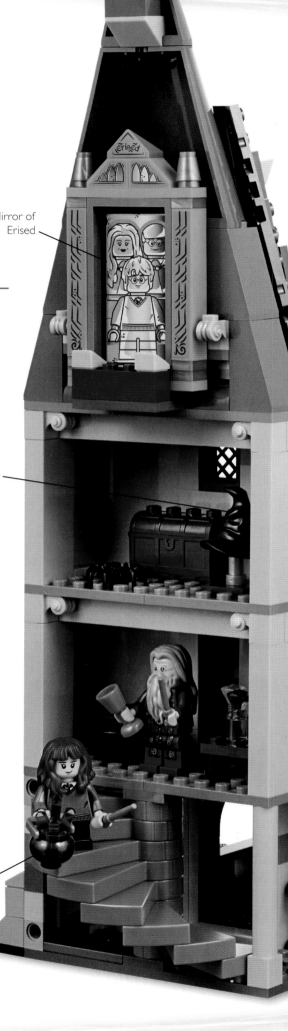

Mirror of Erised

The Sorting Hat

Hermione carries Potions cauldron

SPIRALING STAIRCASE

Here, minifigures can pass between the ground floor and the Potions room—if the moving stairs allow it! Threaded onto a column, the steps can be stacked or fanned into a spiral. When the steps are tucked in, Filch's broom cupboard is revealed.

Folds in the hat create a face

⋀ THE SORTING HAT

Upon arriving at Hogwarts, every student is put into one of the school's four houses by the magical Sorting Hat. The scruffy hat is as ancient as Hogwarts itself, and it's incredibly wise at determining which house each student is best suited to. It also gives sage advice—to those willing to listen.

SCHOOL LIFE

The Great Hall, with its large fireplace, is where students gather three times a day to eat meals. It's also where announcements are made and special feast celebrations are held. It is a good job there's plenty of room, as the set comes with ten minifigures, including Professor Quirrell and Susan Bones.

DUELING CLUB

During Harry's second year, the Defense Against the Dark Arts teacher is celebrity wizard Gilderoy Lockhart. He starts a club for students to practice their dueling skills in the Great Hall, but like most of his ideas, it ends in chaos. Poor Justin Finch-Fletchley faces a dangerous snake.

Set name *Hogwarts Great Hall*	
Year 2018	**Number** 75954
Pieces 878	**Minifigures** 10

Owls deliver post to the Great Hall

"Floating" candles

House banners are double-sided

Harry battles Draco in a Dueling Club encounter

40 square window grilles are included in the set

Professor McGonagall sits at the teachers' table

Susan Bones enjoys a cup of tea

ALBUS DUMBLEDORE

Nobody embodies Hogwarts School of Witchcraft and Wizardry as much as its Headmaster, Albus Percival Wulfric Brian Dumbledore. He is a wizard of great power and wisdom. His kindly smile and twinkling eyes reassure his students, but he is no pushover.

Gold half-moon glasses

⌃ HOGWARTS HEADMASTER

In the Hogwarts Great Hall (set 75954), Dumbledore's distinguished minifigure wears rich maroon robes with printed metallic whirls to give a touch of magic. He sports the untied, free-flowing version of his beard.

Beard printing on face

◄ DANCING DUMBLEDORE

On the Christmas Eve of Harry's fourth year, Dumbledore dresses in his fanciest lavender robes for the Yule Ball. He enjoys the celebration with a friendly, relaxed face. If anything should go wrong, his head can be turned around to look concerned—or perhaps tired after dancing the night away!

Embroidered gold edging

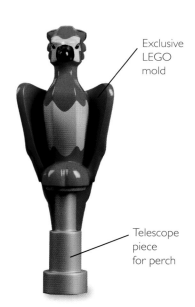

Exclusive LEGO mold

Telescope piece for perch

Hat with a gold tassel is molded to a new hair piece

➤ THOUGHTFUL WIZARD

Anyone who peers into the swirling contents of a Pensieve will be sucked into the memory stored within it. Dumbledore keeps a large, stone Pensieve in his office and his minifigure, in embroidered blue robes, holds a version of it here.

FAWKES THE PHOENIX

Fawkes is a scarlet Phoenix who lives in Dumbledore's office. When Phoenixes die, they burst into flames and are then reborn from their own ashes. This is adult Fawkes—a young Phoenix appears in Dumbledore's Office (set 76402).

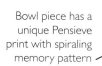

Bowl piece has a unique Pensieve print with spiraling memory pattern

Instead of leg[s] Dumbledore has an elegan[t] curved LEGO slope piece f[or] his long robe[s]

DUMBLEDORE'S OFFICE

Dumbledore's large study is such an important room that it features in more than one LEGO set. In this large set, it's the main attraction, expanding over three storys. In his office, Dumbledore gives Harry one-to-one lessons to prepare him for future challenges.

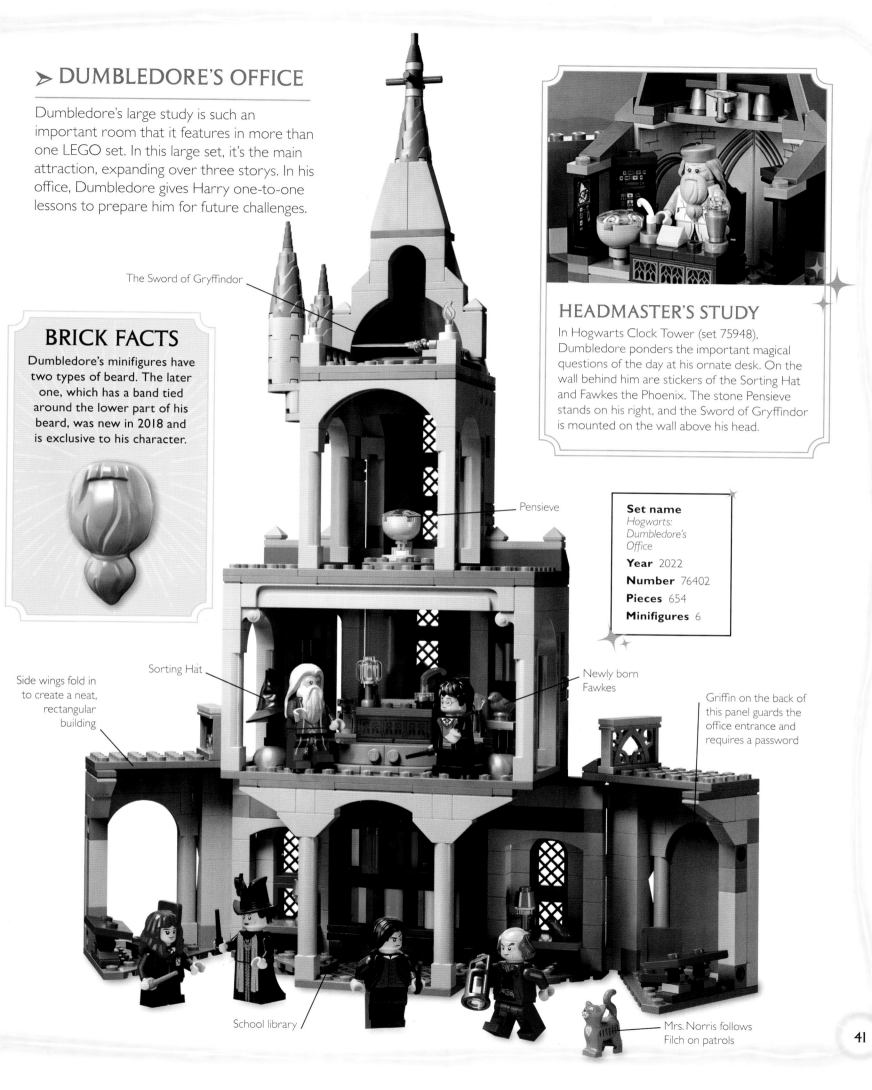

The Sword of Gryffindor

BRICK FACTS

Dumbledore's minifigures have two types of beard. The later one, which has a band tied around the lower part of his beard, was new in 2018 and is exclusive to his character.

HEADMASTER'S STUDY

In Hogwarts Clock Tower (set 75948), Dumbledore ponders the important magical questions of the day at his ornate desk. On the wall behind him are stickers of the Sorting Hat and Fawkes the Phoenix. The stone Pensieve stands on his right, and the Sword of Gryffindor is mounted on the wall above his head.

Pensieve

Set name	
Hogwarts: Dumbledore's Office	
Year	2022
Number	76402
Pieces	654
Minifigures	6

Sorting Hat

Side wings fold in to create a neat, rectangular building

Newly born Fawkes

Griffin on the back of this panel guards the office entrance and requires a password

School library

Mrs. Norris follows Filch on patrols

41

WITHIN HOGWARTS

Hogwarts castle is bolstered by powerful spells and charms—some of which even Dumbledore hasn't uncovered. Bathilda Bagshot's book *Hogwarts: A History* reveals interesting details about the castle—for example, that the Great Hall's ceiling is enchanted to look like the sky outside. But there are still plenty of secrets for Harry and his friends to discover for themselves as they explore the ancient castle.

➤ ARCHITECTURE IN MINIATURE

Although this LEGO set is built to microscale, it captures the grandeur of Hogwarts castle, with high ceilings, Roman and Gothic arches, colorful stained glass, ornate stonework, and soaring spires. The rooms, scenes, and characters within are inspired by Harry's first five years at Hogwarts.

HOSPITAL WING

Madam Pomfrey cares for students and staff who are taken ill or suffer an unfortunate accident. In the Hospital Wing (set 76398), she has magical potions and charms, but some injuries, like Ron's broken leg, still take time to repair with Skele-Gro.

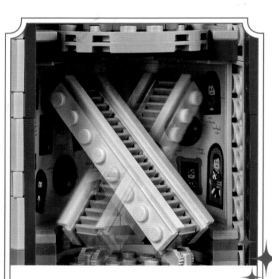

SPINNING STAIRCASES

It's hard enough for students to find their way around the vast castle—and that's without the stairs turning against them! Hogwarts is famous for its 142 enchanted staircases that move at will. Thanks to turntables and hinged connections, these stairs can completely change direction, too.

Writing on the wall says "The Chamber of Secrets has been opened. Enemies of the heir beware."

Set name	*Hogwarts Castle*	
Year 2018	**Number** 71043	
Pieces 6,020	**Minifigures** 4 (plus 27 microfigures)	

Bellatrix Lestrange lurks in the Room of Requirement

➤ OWLERY

In its remote location, Hogwarts is dependent on the Owl Post to know what's going on in the outside world. Hogwarts' Owlery is a dedicated tower, where students' owls can live, and visiting owls can rest between long journeys. It can be a chilly place because it's open for the owls to fly in and out—or if you ask someone to the Yule Ball and they turn you down.

Portraits of former headteachers

Set name	*The Owlery*	
Year 2024		**Number** 76430
Pieces 364		**Minifigures** 3

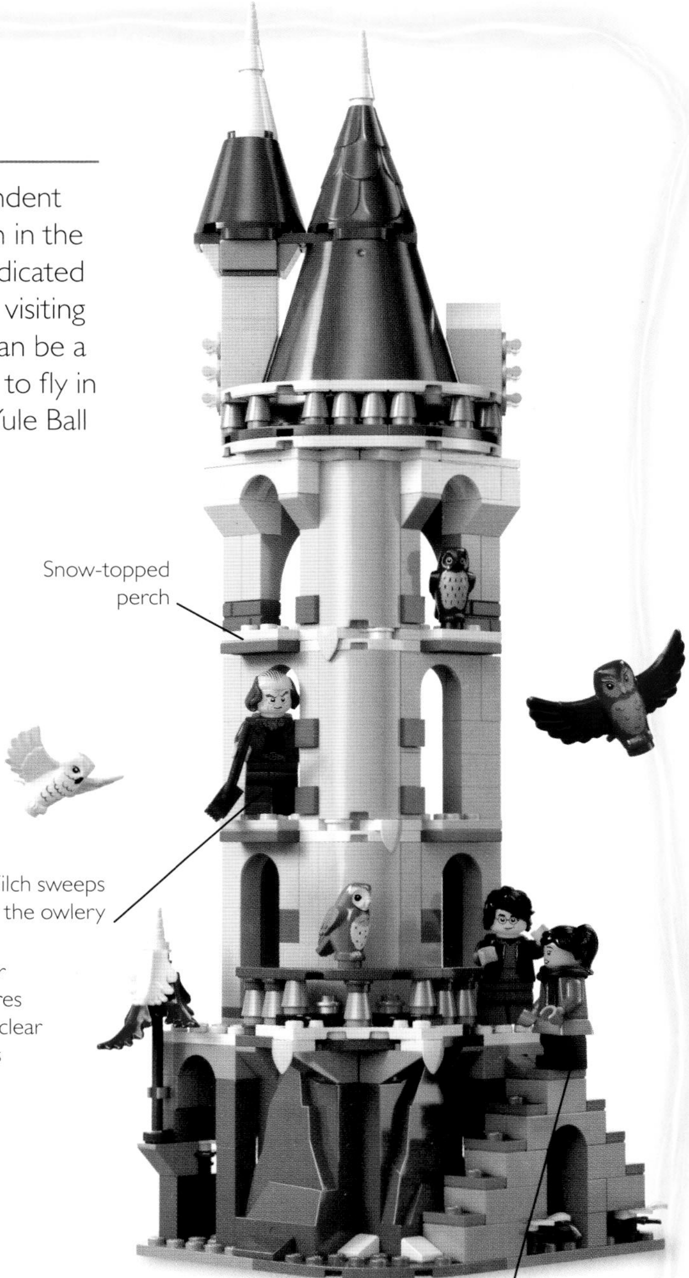

Snow-topped perch

Filch sweeps the owlery

Dragon skeleton hangs on classroom wall

Griffin statue outside Dumbledore's study

Dementor microfigures patrol on clear bar pieces

Cho Chang is wrapped up against the cold

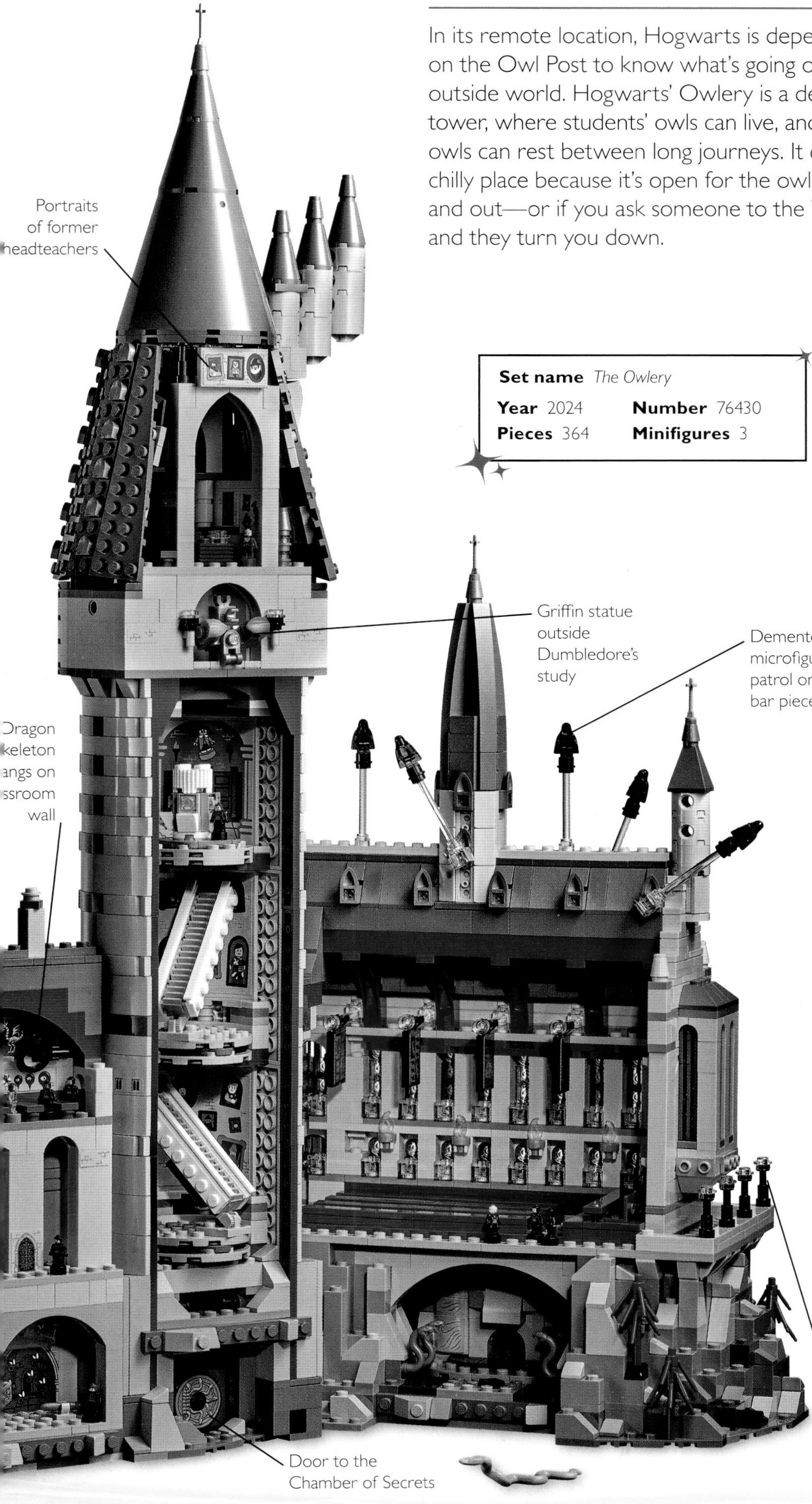

BRICK FACTS

This piece was originally used by minifigures as a ski pole, but here it's mint-green and turned upside down. It tops each of Hogwarts' spires, fitting into a small cone to connect it to the larger turrets.

Door to the Chamber of Secrets

Telescope piece makes a lamppost

Oversized moleskin coat

RUBEUS HAGRID

Towering over other minifigures, this half-giant and half-wizard is Rubeus Hagrid—Keeper of Keys and Grounds at Hogwarts. He may seem rather gruff, but really he is a sensitive soul who sees the gentle side of all creatures (even those others would find alarming!). Hagrid takes Harry under his wing and is fiercely loyal to both him and to Dumbledore.

BRICK FACTS

Hagrid's shaggy mass of brown hair swamps his regular-sized minifigure head. His eyes peek out through the single hair-moustache-and-beard piece, which isn't seen on any other character.

△ GENTLE GIANT

Hagrid's LEGO figure clips together differently from standard minifigures. He has short unposeable legs, but he stands taller thanks to his large, custom-made body piece. He appears in sets with his hut, the Great Hall, Diagon Alley, and Hogsmeade Station because he helps the first years there.

∨ HAGRID'S HUT

After work, Hagrid doesn't need to leave his beloved Hogwarts because he has his own cozy home in the castle grounds. His eight-sided hut is built as two LEGO half-rooms, opened up for easy playing. Inside, Hagrid's tools hang from the rafters, and the fireplace glows with a brick that really lights up.

SECRET SPELLMAKER?

Hagrid hasn't been allowed to do magic with a wand since he was expelled from Hogwarts and his wand was broken. However, it's rumored that he carries the wand pieces around with him, hidden inside his pink umbrella.

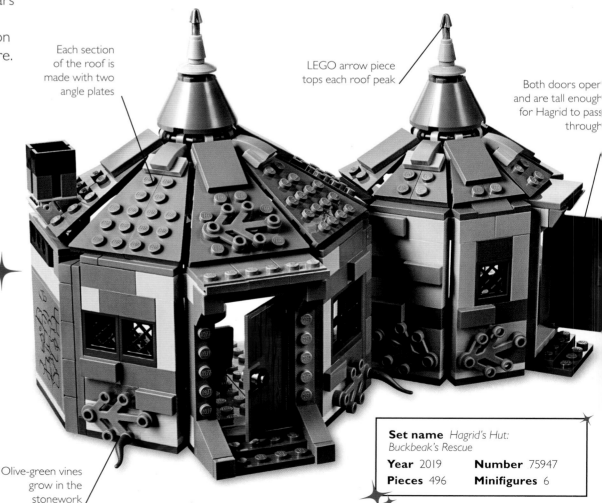

Each section of the roof is made with two angle plates

LEGO arrow piece tops each roof peak

Both doors open and are tall enough for Hagrid to pass through

Olive-green vines grow in the stonework

Set name *Hagrid's Hut: Buckbeak's Rescue*

Year 2019	**Number** 75947
Pieces 496	**Minifigures** 6

GOOD FRIEND

Kind Hagrid helps Harry navigate the wizarding world. After delivering the news that Harry's a wizard, Hagrid takes him shopping in Diagon Alley. Before the second year, Harry accidentally winds up in Knockturn Alley, but Hagrid is on hand to rescue him.

TIME FOR TEA

Harry, Ron, and Hermione are always welcome in Hagrid's hut. It's a cozy place to chat, so long as they don't mind spiders in the rafters and a dragon egg in the fireplace. Hagrid can be a useful source of information even if he doesn't always mean to be.

Furry dress robes with extra-furry trim

Large polka-dot tie isn't Hagrid's usual style

Refreshing cup of tea

▼ ANIMAL SANCTUARY

Hagrid feels great affinity with all living creatures. Even sharp claws, snarling teeth, or lethal clumsiness don't put him off. His second Hut (set 76428) includes the first mold of his giant boarhound, Fang. Also, the dragon he was incubating with a glowing LEGO brick in his first Hut (set 75947) has now hatched!

◄ DRESSED TO IMPRESS

Even Hagrid makes an effort to dress up sometimes. He swaps his moleskin overcoat for furry old dress robes, a shirt, and a polka-dot tie to greet Madame Maxime in Beauxbatons' Carriage: Arrival at Hogwarts (set 75958). He still looks rather scruffy, but he is very warm and welcoming.

Opened-out set folds up into an octagon

Norbert's egg

Norbert freshly hatched

Fang

Insulated clothing to protect Hagrid from Norbert

Set name
Hagrid's Hut
Year 2024
Number 76428
Pieces 896
Minifigures 5

HOGWARTS' GROUNDS

Hogwarts was built in a remote location, away from prying Muggle eyes. Apart from the small village of Hogsmeade, there is no one around for miles, but it's not a boring place. The countryside is perfect for studying magical plants and creatures in their natural habitats. But, minifigures must be careful: Hogwarts' grounds are not always safe.

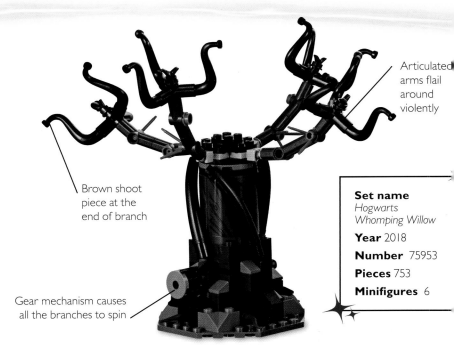

Articulated arms flail around violently

Brown shoot piece at the end of branch

Gear mechanism causes all the branches to spin

Set name
Hogwarts Whomping Willow
Year 2018
Number 75953
Pieces 753
Minifigures 6

GRAWP THE GIANT

The Forbidden Forest is a useful place to hide things, like Hagrid's "baby" half-brother, Grawp. Hagrid is trying to teach the brutish young giant to be less aggressive, but it doesn't seem to be working.

1x2 jumper plate for tummy button

Set name
Forbidden Forest: Umbridge's Encounter
Year 2020
Number 75967
Pieces 253
Minifigures 3

⋀ THE WHOMPING WILLOW

The magical Whomping Willow lashes out at anything within whacking distance. Planted to protect a secret entrance to the Shrieking Shack, the tree's vicious, whirling branches will attack anyone who comes near enough.

➤ THE FORBIDDEN FOREST

Stay away from the Forbidden Forest. It bristles with magic and many dangers lurk among its dark trees. The area is strictly out of bounds to students—unless they're serving detention with a teacher.

Set name *Forbidden Forest*	
Year 2024	**Number** 76432
Pieces 172	**Minifigures** 2

Buckbeak the Hippogriff

Cornish Pixie

Baby Thestral

➤ THE BLACK LAKE

The Hogwarts Express brings pupils to Hogsmeade Station, but there's further to go to reach the castle. First-years cross the deep, icy waters of the Black Lake in small brick-built boats. No one needs to row—the boats magically move themselves. Professor McGonagall is on the shore to welcome the students.

Set name	Hogwarts Castle Boathouse	
Year 2024	**Number** 76426
Pieces 350	**Minifigures** 5

Tower introduces a new building color to the modular Hogwarts system

Flambeaux are mini flames in tubes with bars that fit into clips in the wall

Sitting minifigures connect to studs in the bottom of the boat

Neville sits behind Harry

BRICK FACTS

Luna Lovegood's minifigures often carry *The Quibbler*—the newspaper her father edits. She is an avid reader, but most wizards and witches regard its stories as sensational nonsense.

▼ CARRIAGE RIDE

After their first year, students travel to the castle from Hogsmeade station on special carriages. To most, they appear to be propeled by magic, but those who have seen death can see that the carriages are pulled by black skeletal Thestrals.

Seating for four minifigures

Fleshless, bony body

Harry first sees the Thestrals in his fifth year

Baby Thestrals' wings are molded to body

Thin, glossy leatherlike coat

Meat for feeding Thestral

Set name	
Hogwarts Carriage and Thestrals	
Year 2022	
Number 76400	
Pieces 121	
Minifigures 2	

THE SHRIEKING SHACK

A dilapidated house in Hogsmeade, the Shrieking Shack is believed by locals to be haunted. The building was a hideout for Hogwarts student Remus Lupin to spend time when he turned into a werewolf. The house was a sanctuary for his own protection as well as the safety of all witches, wizards, Muggles, and any local wildlife.

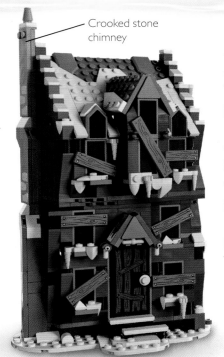

Crooked stone chimney

◄ SAFE HOUSE

The front of the tilted, wonky house is not a welcoming sight. Boarded up windows, a crumbling door, and icicles hanging from the derelict windowsills are all part of the plan to keep people away. Rumors of hauntings also stop people investigating and putting themselves in danger.

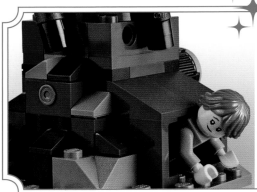

SECRET TUNNEL

To reach the Shrieking Shack from the school there is a secret tunnel as seen in Hogwarts Whomping Willow (set 75953). The violent willow tree was planted to hide the entrance and keep people away by attacking anyone who approaches.

Set name	The Shrieking Shack & Whomping Willow	
Year 2022		**Number** 76407
Pieces 777		**Minifigures** 6

➤OLD HAUNT

During Harry's third year, the Shrieking Shack is the scene for an epic confrontation and unexpected revelations: Azkaban prison escapee Sirius Black is innocent! Ron's pet rat Scabbers is actually Peter Pettigrew! He has been hiding for 12 years since betraying Harry's parents to Lord Voldemort and framing Sirius for his crimes.

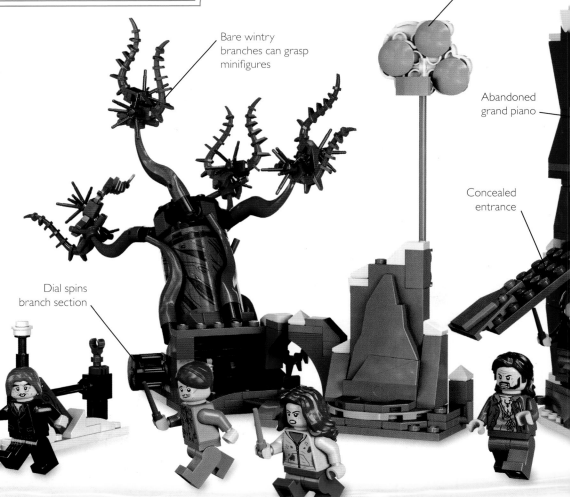

Cloudy sky

Bare wintry branches can grasp minifigures

Abandoned grand piano

Concealed entrance

Dial spins branch section

Telescope piece

Skeleton leg piece in brown

DANGEROUS TREE

Hermione is grabbed by the Whomping Willow when she gets too close. It grasps her in its tentaclelike branches and flings her around in the air. At least her minifigure can get checked over by Madam Pomfrey in Hogwarts Hospital Wing (set 76398).

Scars inflicted as a werewolf

Tatty prison clothes

Ratlike features

◄ THE MARAUDERS

When Harry Potter's dad, James, was at Hogwarts, he and his three friends —Remus Lupin, Sirius Black, and Peter Pettigrew—called themselves the Marauders. They protected Remus each month when he turned into a werewolf and they kept his secret. However, Peter later betrayed them all to Voldemort.

➤ ANIMAGUS

Aside from Remus (nick-named "Moony"), who was a werewolf, each Marauder became an Animagus. James ("Prongs") was a stag; Peter ("Wormtail") a rat; and Sirius ("Padfoot") a black dog, which is in this set.

Printed fur detail

BRICK FACTS

This 2x4 Marauder's Map tile shows Draco's location. The magical object was designed by the Marauders to reveal where everyone in Hogwarts is.

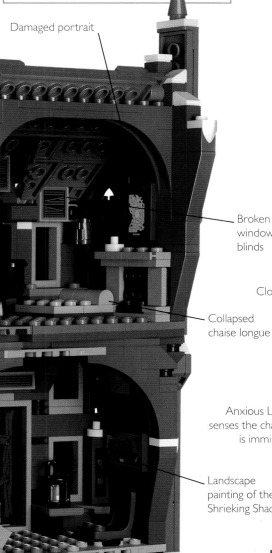

Damaged portrait

Broken window blinds

Collapsed chaise longue

Cloud-covered moon

Full moon LEGO piece glows in the dark

◄ TERRIBLE TRANSFORMATION

Once a month, Lupin transforms into a ferocious werewolf with no memory of his humanity. This LEGO build swivels to swap minifigures for the frightful transformation—and once again to return him to his human minifigure form once the ordeal is over.

Anxious Lupin senses the change is imminent

Landscape painting of the Shrieking Shack

Lupin fully transformed

Turntable piece swivels rocky section

Model attaches to the Whomping Willow build

Red version of Nearly Headless Nick and Ollivander's hair

GRYFFINDOR HOUSE

More than 1,000 years ago, four witches and wizards came together to establish Hogwarts. Each founder gave their name to a house that celebrates key aspects of their personality. Godric Gryffindor created his house for those with the traits of courage, bravery, and determination. It's no surprise that Harry, Ron, and Hermione are all Gryffindors!

HOUSE BANNER

The 2023 common room sets fold up into 3D house flags that can be hung on the wall. Gryffindor's lion stands rampant against the red-and-gold house colors

⚡ GODRIC GRYFFINDOR

As bold and brave as a lion, Hogwarts founder Godric Gryffindor also looks a little like his house's symbol, with his bushy, manelike hair and beard. He faced every situation with great courage and valued bravery and determination. His minifigure holds his dueling wand in one hand and the legendary Sword of Gryffindor in the other.

➤ COMMON ROOM

Gryffindor is the first of the four common room sets that reflect the character of each house. As well as folding up, every set has a backdrop with images visible through gaps in the LEGO wall. The lenticular images move— as if by magic! In one image, Sirius Black's face appears in the fire to talk to Harry.

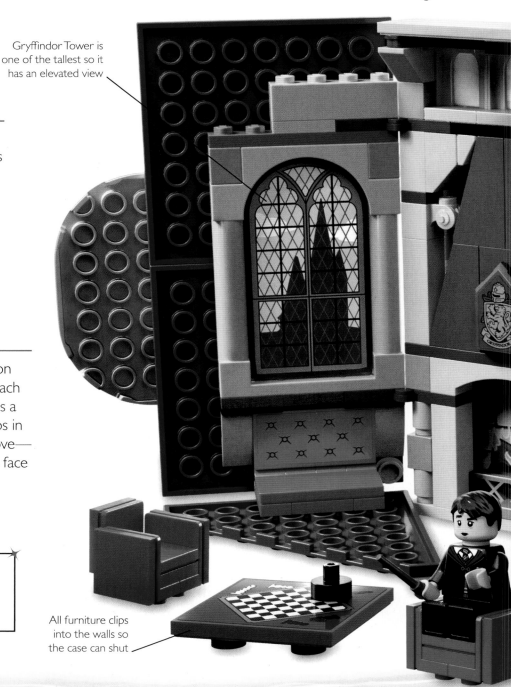

Gryffindor Tower is one of the tallest so it has an elevated view

All furniture clips into the walls so the case can shut

Set name	*Gryffindor House Banner*	
Year 2023	**Number** 76409	
Pieces 285	**Minifigures** 3	

Traditional witch's hat

◄ PROFESSOR MCGONAGALL

Transfiguration teacher Minerva McGonagall is the head of Gryffindor House. Firm but fair, she doesn't allow any nonsense from anyone. Students occasionally feel her wrath and she isn't afraid to stand up to officials who interfere with the running of the school, either. She's stern but can show great warmth to the pupils under her care.

Emerald-green robes with leg piece rather than skirt

NIGHT OWLS

Hogwarts Gryffindor Dorms (set 40452) has wall space for 16 chocolate frog tiles and two four-poster beds for Ron and Harry's minifigures from Hogwarts Whomping Willow (set 75953). A gift with purchase, the modular build can attach to other Hogwarts sets with LEGO® Technic pins.

Quidditch Cup flickers between "1" and "4"

Flying Thestral sometimes visible in sky

Spiral staircase leads to dormitories

Angelina Johnson

Sword of Gryffindor

NEVILLE LONGBOTTOM

The Sorting Hat saw something in shy, unsure Neville that most people didn't. It knew that he was a bold, brave, true Gryffindor.

Medium-sized poseable leg piece

PARVATI PATIL

Occasionally family members are sorted into different houses, but more often they follow each other, just like Parvati and her twin Padma.

Muggle clothes for trip to Hogsmeade

DEAN THOMAS

Brave and loyal Dean is a classic Gryffindor. With his good nature, he gets along well with everyone and is friends with Harry.

Expression of pure childlike joy

COLIN CREEVEY

Young Colin is very excited to join the same house as his hero—Harry Potter! Colin is in the year below Harry so has short legs.

Badger symbol on clasp of cape

Hufflepuff cup later became a Horcrux

Robes are elegant but not showy

HUFFLEPUFF HOUSE

Dedication, patience, and loyalty are some of the qualities associated with students in yellow-and-black Hufflepuff House. Thanks to their focus on hard work and honesty, they develop their varied talents and acheive successes in a wide range of fields. Renowned Hufflepuffs include the famous magizoologist Newt Scamander and the Triwizard star Cedric Diggory.

HOUSE BANNER

The bold badger marks out the Hufflepuff crest c its striking yellow-and-blac flag. The common room set folds up and can be hung up as a banner.

Set name	*Hufflepuff House Banner*	
Year 2023	**Number** 76412	
Pieces 313	**Minifigures** 3	

⌃ HELGA HUFFLEPUFF

While her fellow teachers concerned themselves with teaching the cleverest or the most courageous, Helga Hufflepuff just wanted her students to be fair and loyal and to apply themselves. In return, she offered them equally fair treatment, saying, "I'll teach the lot and treat them just the same."

Former student Newt Scamander and his Niffler

➤ COMMON ROOM

The warm tan walls and cheerful yellow of the Hufflepuff common room reflect the house's kind, welcoming nature. The lenticular background includes paintings of Helga Hufflepuff, a Mimbulus mimbletonia, a Mandrake, and Devil's Snare. On each side of the fireplace, a sneaky Niffler searches for and snaffles a golden coin.

LEGO plant piece was new in 2022

Plant accessories

Ear defenders protect from the harmful sound of Mandrakes

Mud on overalls

⌃ PROFESSOR SPROUT

During Harry's time, the Head of Hufflepuff is cheerful Professor Pomona Sprout. Her love of her subject Herbology is evident in the common room set: from the oil paintings of plants and vegetation growing up the walls to lush produce on the floor, and tools like pruning shears and a watering can.

JUSTIN FINCH-FLETCHLEY

As a second-year with short non-poseable legs, Justin Finch-Fletchley appears in Hogwarts Chamber of Secrets (set 76389).

Moaning Myrtle's pigtail mold now in reddish brown

SUSAN BONES

Older than her first minifigure and now with pigtails, Susan Bones looks either worried or relaxed in Hufflepuff House Banner (set 76412).

Blonde version of Rowena Ravenclaw's hair piece

HANNAH ABBOTT

Since her first minifigure in Hogwarts Students Accessory Set (set 40419), Hannah now has her hair down and black robes over her Hufflepuff sweater.

Torso shared with Hannah Abbott (far right)

Table clips in here to be folded away

Wooden barrels in wall

Hufflepuff's Cup

53

Diadem was later lost for centuries

Starry-night pattern

RAVENCLAW HOUSE

Following in the footsteps of their founder, Rowena Ravenclaw, students in Ravenclaw House value the traits of wit, learning, and wisdom. They are often clever, curious, creative, and diligent, so they tend to excel in their studies. As the Sorting Hat says, if you've a ready mind, wise old Ravenclaw is where you'll always find your kind.

HOUSE BANNER

The common room set fo studious Ravenclaws folds up into a blue-and-gray display banner with their house emblem, the raven with a silver-printed beak.

⌃ ROWENA RAVENCLAW

An exceptionally clever witch, Rowena Ravenclaw favored students with the sharpest minds. The values of learning and wisdom live on in Ravenclaws today, who follow the motto engraved onto their founder's diadem: "Wit beyond measure is man's greatest treasure." She had a daughter, Helena, who became the Ravenclaw ghost, the Gray Lady.

➤ COMMON ROOM

Pale stone and rich blue walls make Ravenclaw's common room a calm place to study. The lenticular sheet shows Rowena Ravenclaw's statue and large windows for plenty of blue-sky thinking. A hidden noticeboard has Luna's list of lost (or stolen) things.

Crannies full of books

Muggle-style dress shirt

Triangular floor pieces double as points of the banner

➤ PROFESSOR FLITWICK

The Head of Ravenclaw is part-goblin so all Filius Flitwick's minifigures have short leg pieces. However, between Harry's second and third years, other aspects of Flitwick's appearance changes. Here, in Harry's third year, Flitwick is dressed smartly, but in LEGO® Harry Potter™ Advent Calendar (set 75964), he has taken off his jacket for some festive frivolity.

Bare shirt sleeves normally under black jacket

RELAXATION TIME

Luna reads the newspaper in her Ravenclaw dormitory after Professor Slughorn's Slug Club party in Hogwarts Astronomy Tower (set 75969). Her minifigure wears a festive Christmas tree-inspired dress.

2021 uniform torso design

CHO CHANG

Cho's second-year minifigure from Hogwarts Moment: Charms Class (set 76385) shows great intelligence as well as potential as a Quidditch player.

Quirky Spectrespecs

LUNA LOVEGOOD

Many regard Luna's way of thinking and looking at the world as strange, but it gives her an intelligence that is appreciated by Ravenclaw House.

Harry wears a similar design in Gryffindor colors

MICHAEL CORNER

A clever Ravenclaw and member of Dumbledore's Army, Michael's minifigure is the first to have a Ravenclaw torso with a tie and cardigan combo.

Hoop for hanging set up

Set name	*Ravenclaw House Banner*	
Year 2023		**Number** 76411
Pieces 305		**Minifigures** 3

BRICK FACTS

In Hogwarts Great Hall (set 75954), the blue-and-gray Ravenclaw banner with ravens hangs down over the long dining tables.

Clip for storing Cho's book

Cornish Pixie

Reading lamps pack up into the arch on the left

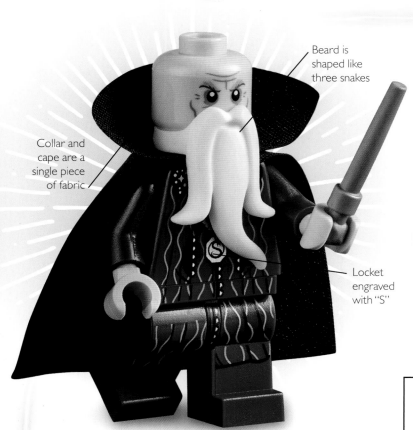

Beard is shaped like three snakes

Collar and cape are a single piece of fabric

Locket engraved with "S"

SLYTHERIN HOUSE

Despite its reputation, Slytherin House isn't all about the Dark Arts. More commonly, Slytherin students are known for the traits of pride, ambition, and cunning. They will do whatever it takes to acheive their goals, and they make strong leaders, but it is true that the house has had more than its fair share of the cruelest wizards and witches.

HOUSE BANNER

The curved snake with a forked tongue, favored by Salazar Slytherin, identifies Slytherin House, along with the serpentine house colors of green and silver.

Set name	Slytherin House Banner	
Year 2023		**Number** 76410
Pieces 349		**Minifigures** 3

⌃ SALAZAR SLYTHERIN

Salazar Slytherin sought out the most ambitious and talented for his house. He only wanted students from pureblood wizarding families. His desire to close Hogwarts to anyone Muggle-born caused a split with the other founders. Before he left, he built the Chamber of Secrets with the monstrous Basilisk.

Eerie transparent green bricks

Fold-out steps lead to and from entrance

Creepy lenticular eye blinks

➤ COMMON ROOM

Deep in the dungeons, Slytherin's common room looks out into the watery depths of the Black Lake. In the cupboard, a notorius Slytherin student has graffitied "Tom Riddle was here." The cold, gray-stone room is filled with Dark artifacts like a skull, dubious potions, and a Hand of Glory.

Snake details also used in the Chamber of Secrets (set 76389)

Fierce expression is slightly less cross on the other side

Wand is used to help Harry in Quidditch Match (set 75956)

▲ PROFESSOR SNAPE

Head of Slytherin House, Severus Snape embodies two of Harry's least favorite things about school: Slytherin enemies and Snape himself. The Potions master is an imposing figure, even in LEGO form, and he appears to revel in making Harry's life miserable. However, he has been known to help Harry out in a crisis.

⋁ TOM RIDDLE

Fifty years before Harry Potter's time at Hogwarts, there was a Slytherin student called Tom Marvolo Riddle. Clever, charming, and calculating, this seemingly popular boy went on to become the Darkest wizard the world has ever known.

Old-fashioned Slytherin robes

Portrait of Severus Snape

Dangerous Hand of Glory

Pet snakes appeal to Slytherin students

Hair can be swapped for Ron's

VINCENT CRABBE

Vincent Crabbe and his friend, Gregory Goyle, are Draco's sidekicks. They're generally found following him around and doing what he tells them.

Alternate face print is Harry's

GREGORY GOYLE

Goyle's minifigure, like Crabbe's, can be changed. In Hogwarts: Polyjuice Potion Mistake (set 76386), Ron and Harry pose as these Slytherins.

First Slytherin torso with a Quidditch sweater

BLAISE ZABINI

A keen Quidditch player, Blaise is the Slytherin Chaser. His views on Muggle-borns chimes with Salazar Slytherin's—though Blaise is contemptuous of most other witches and wizards, too.

Torso design is unique to this minifigure

PANSY PARKINSON

The first female Slytherin minifigure, Pansy Parkinson is a friend of Draco's. In Slytherin House Banner (set 76410), she practices charms—is she dabbling with the Dark Arts?

57

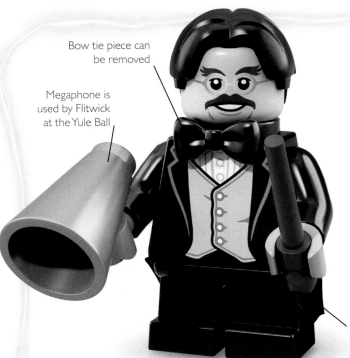

Bow tie piece can be removed

Megaphone is used by Flitwick at the Yule Ball

Fabric coat tails touch the ground

HOGWARTS STAFF

Teachers are an important part of the Hogwarts school community, living and working in the school for many years. The wizarding world can be overwhelming to young wizards and witches. There's so much to learn! Students don't want to muddle up Spleenwart with Sneezewort or fail to recognize exploding Erumpent fluid. Hogwarts staff are here to help—though some more so than others.

CHOIR MASTER

In the LEGO Harry Potter Advent Calendar (set 75964), Professor Flitwick has taken off his jacket so he can conduct the Hogwarts festive choir more easily. His open mouth sings along merrily with his students.

◢ PROFESSOR FLITWICK

Filius Flitwick is as intelligent as you'd expect the head of Ravenclaw House to be. He's an expert Charms master as well as a dueling champion. Part-goblin, his minifigures have short, unposeable legs, and he's always very smartly dressed in a three-piece suit, dress shirt, and bow tie.

➤ FILCH

The caretaker Argus Filch is happiest when he's prowling the corridors with his cat, Mrs. Norris, to gleefully get students into trouble. Under bushy eyebrows, his eyes are on constant lookout for rule-breakers. He wears a long, gray overcoat to protect his clothes from dust and dirt.

Bald patch and hair attach on top of head as a single piece

Scruffy waistcoat

BRICK FACTS

Filch's cat, Mrs. Norris, loyally follows her master and likes to get students in trouble, too. She shares a LEGO mold with Hermione's cat, Crookshanks, but has a unique coloring.

HIGHWAY PATROL

In Hogwarts Whomping Willow (set 75953), Filch paces the castle ramparts with a lantern hoping to find students who have snuck out of bed. However, when he does catch delinquents, he's always disappointed by the school's "soft" punishments— he would be harsher!

Keys to Hogwarts

MADAM POMFREY

Matronly head cover keeps hair back

Nurse's-style timepiece

Chart for recording patient's vital signs

Doctors are for Muggles—the wizarding world has Healers, like Poppy Pomfrey. As matron of Hogwarts, she oversees the care of all students and staff, treating their magical maladies and mishaps with potions, magical herbs, charms, and a kind bedside manner.

HEALING HANDS

One of Madam Pomfrey's patients is Harry Potter. In Hogwarts Hospital Wing (set 76398), she treats him with Skele-Gro after his arm loses all of its bones because of a magical blunder. He stays under her care overnight while his bones regrow.

Feather piece clips into witch's hat

Black fur stole

Long green-and-gold scarf

◄ MADAM PINCE

Irma Pince takes her job of Hogwarts Librarian very seriously. She's happy to help students search for information, but care of her books comes first. She's very strict when it comes to the rules, and the peace and serenity of her library.

LIBRARY FAN

Hermione is a regular visitor to Madam Pince's library. In Hogwarts: Dumbledore's Office (set 76402), she browses the books of different colors and sizes. Beware the restricted section though. It holds some surprisingly dangerous books!

Witch's hat and hair are a single piece

Telescope built around a LEGO video camera piece

Star chart

PROFESSOR SINISTRA

Aurora Sinistra is the professor of Astronomy. She teaches Hogwarts' young wizards and witches to chart the movements of celestial bodies across the sky. They must learn the names of the stars, moons, and planets, and homework often involves completing star charts.

HOGWARTS GHOSTS

Not all the residents of Hogwarts are alive. A small number of witches and wizards fully get into the spirit of Hogwarts and stay on at the castle after their death. They lose their solid bodies and become floating, transparent ghosts, but they retain their personalities and memories. Each house has its own resident ghost, plus there are others who hang around, too.

Head clips snugly onto hand

Fifteenth-century style jacket

Ghostly body printed in silver and black over gray

Blue pieces match Myrtle's mood

Tom Riddle's diary hits Myrtle when Ginny throws it away

BRICK FACTS

Nearly Headless Nick's second minifigure from 2021 has extra LEGO ghostliness. He wears his previous outfit, but it's printed on white LEGO pieces that glow in the dark!

⌃ NEARLY HEADLESS NICK

Poor Sir Nicholas de Mimsy-Porpington. Since his execution 500 years ago, he's been called Nearly Headless Nick because his head wasn't completely cut off. However, the minifigure versions of the Ghost of Gryffindor Tower can have his head removed and placed on his hand with the ease of any other LEGO connection.

⌃ MOANING MYRTLE

Myrtle was a Ravenclaw student when the Chamber of Secrets was opened 50 years ago. She now haunts the girls' bathroom on the second floor because that's where the Basilisk slithered from the water pipes and their eyes met.

GRAY MATTER

In the 2022 LEGO Harry Potter Advent Calendar (set 76404), Myrtle's minifigure swaps her blue clothes and hair for ghostly gray.

Hair mold was created specially for Myrtle

Eleventh-century witch's robes

BATH TIME

Myrtle can travel through Hogwart's plumbing system. She pops up in the prefects' bathroom when Harry's taking a bath and helps him solve a clue for the Triwizard Tournament.

➤ THE GRAY LADY

Centuries ago, Helena Ravenclaw grew up in the shadow of her famous mother, Rowena, the founder of Ravenclaw House. Now Helena is the Ghost of Ravenclaw Tower, and some people call her the Gray Lady.

FLYING LESSONS

Flying on a broom is an essential skill for any witch or wizard. Even if a student isn't going to play Quidditch, it's a basic way to get around—especially until they are old enough to get their Disapparation license. First-years learn right away, but not everyone gets off to a flying start. Some have been flying since they were knee-high to a Bowtruckle, but Muggle-borns may have only used brooms for sweeping.

∨ FLYING HIGH

Flying lessons take place outside, next to Hogwarts. The back of this model includes a trophy room for the spoils of Quidditch glories and a storage room for everyone's flying and sports equipment.

Set name
Hogwarts: First Flying Lesson
Year 2021
Number 76395
Pieces 264
Minifigures 4

Levitating broom function uses a clear LEGO pole

Stone statue made with minifigure pieces

All four houses are represented

BRICK FACTS

The first LEGO Harry Potter brooms were based on the LEGO® Fabuland™ design, but 2022 saw the first brick-built broom. It allows for more variation, including LEGO handcuffs for foot stirrups.

➤ MADAM HOOCH

No-nonsense Rolanda Hooch is the Hogwarts flying instructor. Learning to fly on magic broomsticks can be dangerous, and it's not long into the first lesson that she has to take an injured Neville to the hospital wing.

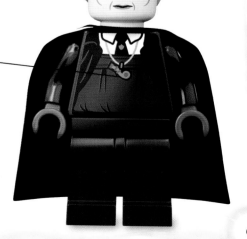

Reverse face wears flying goggles

Whistle to get fliers' attention

TRANSFIGURATION

A particularly difficult branch of magic, Transfiguration is nonetheless a subject that students grapple with early. It concerns the transformation of one object into another. Professor McGonagall starts her class off with the challenge of turning a small creature into a goblet with the incantation *Vera Verto!* Ron achieves some success, but his goblet is furry with a rat's tail sticking out.

Set name
Hogwarts Moment: Transfiguration Class
Year 2021
Number 76382
Pieces 241
Minifigures 3

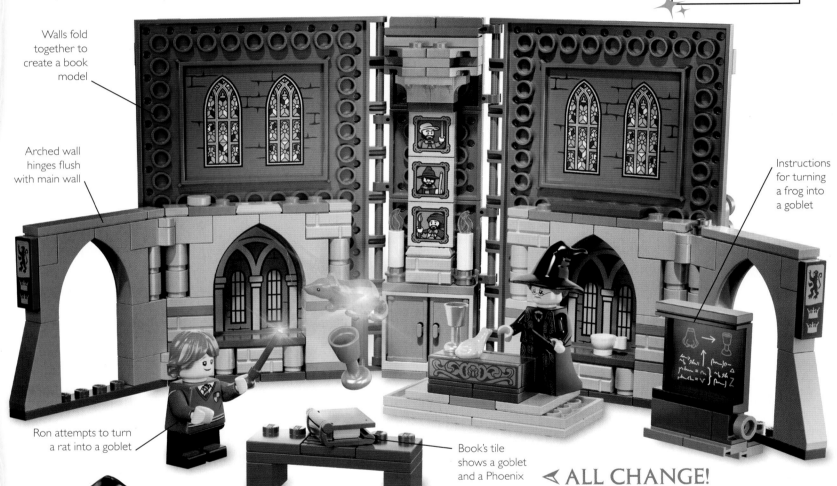

Walls fold together to create a book model

Arched wall hinges flush with main wall

Instructions for turning a frog into a goblet

Ron attempts to turn a rat into a goblet

Book's tile shows a goblet and a Phoenix

Hair attached to witch's hat

Dark green robes do not represent Slytherin!

◄ ALL CHANGE!

Each of the six Hogwarts Moments sets are classrooms, which transfigure into models of large books. The center wall forms the spine, and all the accessories stack inside the book.

◄ SUBJECT EXPERT

Transfiguration is taught by Professor Minerva McGonagall. An Animagus, she can transform herself into a cat at will. She is stern and strict and expects hard work from her students, but she encourages and inspires them.

Arm rests are Slughorn's arms

Head pops up first when Horace starts returning to normal

MASTER OF DISGUISE

With very advanced skills, you can even transfigure yourself. Horace Slughorn hides from Death Eaters as a plush, purple armchair.

CHARMS

One of the most rudimentary skills a witch or wizard needs, Charms is the ability to enchant objects. Professor Flitwick teaches his first-years *Wingardium Leviosa*—a charm to make light, airy feathers rise up and move wherever they're directed. Students must clearly enunciate the incantation while making the correct swish-and-flick movement with their wands.

Beard piece mold first created for LEGO® Lord of the Rings™

◄ CHARMING TEACHER

Charms teacher Professor Filius Flitwick has two types of minifigure based on his different appearances across the films. In Harry's first two years, Professor Flitwick has a white bushy beard and bald head. The short-legged figure stands on his desk to be seen by everyone.

▽ ENCHANTING SCHOOL

Professor Flitwick's classroom is well designed for the study of Charms. Light and airy, it has plenty of space for practical exercises, along with all the books you'd expect the Head of Ravenclaw to have.

Set name
Hogwarts Moment: Charms Class

Year 2021

Number 76385

Pieces 256

Minifigures 3

Ravenclaw's flag representing Flitwick

Harry concentrates on making he feather fly

Cho Chang has a new hair piece

Tile shows the *Wingardium Leviosa* charm

POTIONS

Muggles are familiar with science classes with Bunsen burners and vials of ingredients, but Hogwarts students take brewing concoctions a magical step further. Potions is both a science and an art that can enable witches and wizards to cause an effect on the drinker. Snape could teach a student to "bottle fame, brew glory, and even put a stopper in death." But it's not easy!

∨ DEEP DUNGEON

A Slytherin through and through, Professor Snape teaches in a dungeon decorated with snakes and some hidden graffiti by Tom Riddle. His classroom is packed with ingredients for everything from the truth-telling Veritaserum and Amortentia love potion to the Wolfsbane potion, which relieves symptoms of lycanthropy (werewolfery).

Snape is quick to raise a sneering eyebrow

Supplies of potion ingredients

Latin for "potassium carbonate"

⋀ POTIONS PROFESSOR

Many students get themselves in a stew in Severus Snape's classes—the Potions Professor is quick to sneer and criticise. Although he teaches Potions, everyone knows it's the Defense Against the Arts position that Snape really covets.

➤ CLASS CASUALTY

Poor, clumsy Seamus Finnegan gets on the wrong side of his potion, and it blows up in his face. His minifigure has a double-printed head: one side is covered with soot; the other smiles happily. Perhaps it's from before his mishap, or maybe after he's bounced back from it.

Slightly wrong combination of volatile ingredients

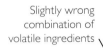

Temporary marks from explosion

Eight 1x2 plates
with bars

Hair piece features
two shades of gray

Well-worn
tweed clothes

Felix Felicis
potion

▲ PROFESSOR SLUGHORN

Students who are gifted at Potions will do well
in Horace Slughorn's jovial classes. But they'll
do even better if the vain and easily flattered
Slughorn thinks that they're a valuable addition
to his collection of Very Important People.
Those who make the grade receive an
invitation to his exclusive Slug Club.

Fireplace for heating
dungeon and
warming potions

Set name
*Hogwarts
Moment: Potions
Class*

Year 2021

Number 76383

Pieces 271

Minifigures 3

...ow table covered in
...umper plates

Clear radar dish

POTIONS MASTER

Professor Slughorn comes
out of retirement and returns
to the post of Potions master
in Harry's sixth year. He
mixes work and leisure in
Hogwarts Astronomy Tower
(set 75969). He studies a
Potions textbook in the
classroom, but also throws
a party, complete with a tasty
chocolate fountain!

Transparent-green
1x1 round studs

MAGICAL INGREDIENTS

Potions draw on the natural wonders of
the wizarding world for their ingredients.
Hogwarts Icons—Collectors' Edition (set
76391) includes powdered root of Asphodel
and Infusion of Wormwood, which are used
in the Draught of Living Death.

LEGO bottle glows
in the dark

FELIX FELICIS

Also known as "Liquid
Luck," Felix Felicis is very
tricky to make, but take
one sip and all your
endeavors will succeed—
until the potion wears off.

DEFENSE AGAINST THE DARK ARTS

Magic is a very powerful force, but unfortunately those with bad intentions can use it, too. Hogwarts students must be prepared for whatever awaits them outside (or even inside!) the school. Whether it's incantations to dispatch pesky Red Caps and Hinkypunks or facing off against the Dark Lord, there's much to learn in Defense Against the Dark Arts class.

◀ UNFORGIVABLE CURSES

The three Unforgivable Curses are the darkest magic students could encounter. *Imperio* puts others under the caster's control; *Crucio* causes torture; and *Avada Kedavra* produces a green flash and instant death.

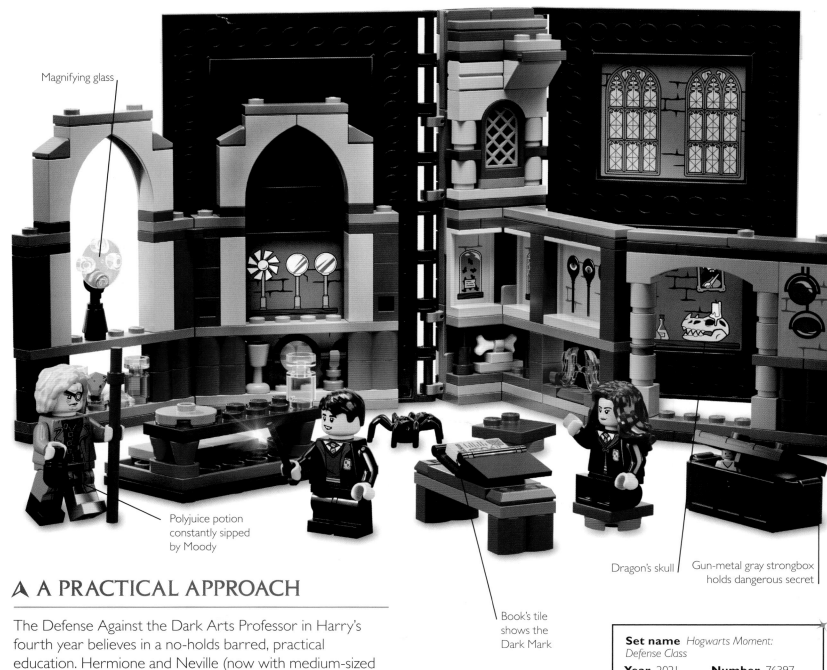

Magnifying glass

Polyjuice potion constantly sipped by Moody

Book's tile shows the Dark Mark

Dragon's skull

Gun-metal gray strongbox holds dangerous secret

▲ A PRACTICAL APPROACH

The Defense Against the Dark Arts Professor in Harry's fourth year believes in a no-holds barred, practical education. Hermione and Neville (now with medium-sized legs), watch as their teacher demonstrates the Unforgivable Curses on a real insectlike creature.

Set name	*Hogwarts Moment: Defense Class*	
Year 2021		**Number** 76397
Pieces 257		**Minifigures** 3

BRICK FACTS

Forewarned is forearmed, so students must know what they're up against. This book shows the Dark Mark—the symbol of Voldemort and his Death Eaters.

BOGGART

Nobody knows what Boggarts actually look like because the shape-shifting creatures take the form of whatever frightens a person the most. For Neville Longbottom, that's Professor Snape. However, a spell to dress the Snape-Boggart in Neville's grandmother's clothes makes it look ridiculous—and far less scary. Boggart defeated!

▼ CORPOREAL PATRONUS

Really advanced Patronus Charms produce not just wisps of vapor or mist but a fully formed corporeal shield in the shape of an animal. Unsurprisingly, Lupin's Patronus is a wolf— but a regular one rather than a werewolf.

Protective shield of positive energy

◀ PATRONUS CHARM

The best defense against Dementors is the Patronus Charm, but it's very advanced magic, way beyond OWL exam level. *Expecto Patronum* creates a positive force that forms a shield against the threat. Professor Lupin tutors Harry in this defensive magic.

▼ MODEL PUPIL

With perserverance and practice on Boggarts, Harry begins to master the Patronus Charm. He has to call upon a fiercely strong, happy memory and concentrate on it, despite his terror of Dementors. What begins as a thin wisp of silvery energy gradually becomes stronger.

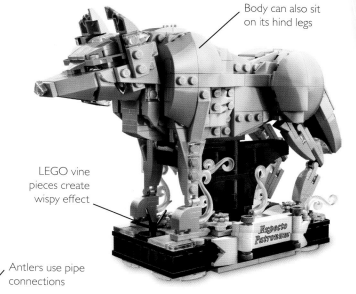

Body can also sit on its hind legs

LEGO vine pieces create wispy effect

Antlers use pipe connections

Set name	*Expecto Patronum*	
Year 2023		**Number** 76414
Pieces 754		**Minifigures** 2

A happy memory powers the charm

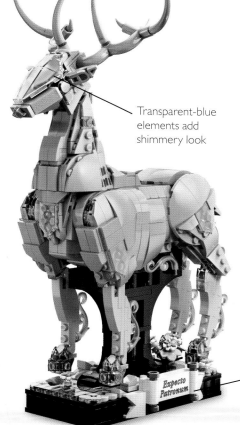

Transparent-blue elements add shimmery look

◀ HARRY'S PATRONUS

Eventually Harry succeeds with a fully corporeal Patronus. His takes the form of a stag, just like his father's did. Coincidentally, Harry's mother, Lily Potter, cast a doe Patronus—as does Severus Snape. Harry's stag comes in Expecto Patronum (set 76414), and its bricks in shades of blue can be reused to build Lupin's wolf Patronus.

Scroll says *Expecto Patronum*

DEFENSE AGAINST THE DARK ARTS PROFESSORS

Ever since Albus Dumbledore refused to hire Tom Riddle as Defense Against the Dark Arts Professor, he has struggled to fill the position. During Harry's time at the school, no teacher of the subject lasts more than a year. It makes for a disrupted curriculum and a wide range of teaching styles. And even some teachers who the students need defending from!

Bags under his eyes from physical strain and worry

Fabric from the turban is draped over his torso and shoulders

➤ QUIRINUS QUIRRELL

In Harry's first year, Professor Quirrell teaches Defense Against the Dark Arts. He has traveled all over the world and adopted elements of the cultures he encountered, including a purple turban. Quirrell uses this headwear to hide Lord Voldemort, who has taken control of his body.

BRICK FACTS

Only Quirrell wears this turban in purple, but the piece has featured on two other minifigures. A Snake Charmer wears it in white and a Desert Warrior in dark green.

➤ GILDEROY LOCKHART

Smile is five-times winner of *Witch Weekly's* Most Charming smile

Lockhart arrives to teach in Harry's second year. He appears to live a gilded life—blessed with accolades like the Order of Merlin Third Class and honorary membership of the Dark Force Defense League. However, he's a fraud and flees when faced with any real danger.

One of many flamboyant, colorful suits

SELF-PROMOTER

Lockhart has a sterling reputation for battling monsters, but it's all lies: he uses memory charms to claim others' glory. Vain Lockhart thrives on fame and adoration. In Hogwarts Chamber of Secrets (set 76389), he loves to sit in his study, signing photographs for his legions of fans. He even gets Harry to help when he's serving detention.

⋀ REMUS LUPIN

Ragged clothes from a tough lifestyle

In Harry's third year, Hogwarts get a talented Professor. He has first-hand experience of the Dark Arts because of his terrible affliction: since being bitten as a child, he's a werewolf. Lupin is an excellent teacher, but becoming a dangerous creature once a month turns out to not be compatible with working in a school.

➤ MAD-EYE MOODY

Flask contains Polyjuice Potion

Artificial eye has magical powers

Alastor "Mad-Eye" Moody is an ex-Auror with a long history fighting the Dark Arts. He would be an excellent choice for Harry's fourth-year Professor, except this isn't Alastor Moody. The Death Eater Barty Crouch Jr. has locked Moody away and taken the teacher's position using Polyjuice Potion. His goal is to get close to Harry to help Voldemort.

TRAPPED

This gunmetal-gray strongbox from Hogwarts Moment: Defense Class (set 76397) contains the real Moody, locked up as a LEGO microfigure.

◄ DOLORES UMBRIDGE

No hair is ever out of place

Brooch with a kitten

Don't be fooled by this friendly looking woman. Underneath the pink, fluffy, frilly clothes and love of kittens, Dolores Umbridge is a cruel, mean witch. She comes to Hogwarts to teach in Harry's fifth year, but she has other dark, secret plans for Hogwarts and its students.

Pink high heels

MINISTRY CLERK

After her disastrous stint at Hogwarts, Umbridge returns to her pink, kitten-filled office in the The Ministry of Magic (set 76403). From here, she doles out her justice to even more people with the cruel Muggle-Born Registration Commission.

Yet another cat brooch

HIGH INQUISITOR

Umbridge delights in dispensing unfair, painful punishments on students. These only increase after she installs herself as Hogwarts High Inquisitor.

HERBOLOGY

A practical knowledge of magical plants is essential so witches and wizards can recognize and use them. Some, like Devil's Snare, are deadly while others are crucial for life-saving potions. Professor Sprout shows her second-years how to repot Mandrakes. The plant's scream can be dangerous and even seedlings can cause a person to faint, so the class must wear protective earmuffs.

Earmuffs are a LEGO earphone piece

GARDEN HELPER

Cedric Diggory is in an older year than Harry's class, but his minifigure is dressed to help Professor Sprout repot Mandrakes in Herbology.

MANDRAKE PREY

Neville has natural flair for Herbology, but that doesn't save him from being knocked out in class—as his alternative sleeping face shows.

➤ HERBOLOGIST

Green-fingered Pomona Sprout, the head of Hufflepuff House, brings her jolliness to teaching Herbology. She loves to potter in the Hogwarts greenhouses, tending to both her plants and her growing students. She hopes they'll all thrive and blossom under her instruction.

Plant-inspired clothing

Secateurs for taking cuttings

Boots on dual-molded legs

▽ GREENHOUSE EFFECT

As well as a lush haven for teaching, Professor Sprout's rooms, overflowing with branches, vines, and leaves, are also productive. She grows valuable potion ingredients like Venomous Tentacula leaves and Mandrakes, which Madam Pomfrey uses in the hospital wing to reverse Petrification.

BRICK FACTS

The baby Mandrake root has a unique mold with a stud on top and a pin underneath. Its wrinkly face print is screaming, but the noise it makes won't be deadly until it's older.

"Be aware" warning sign due to Mandrakes

The Fat Friar, the Hufflepuff Ghost

Set name
Hogwarts Moment: Herbology Class
Year 2021
Number 76384
Pieces 233
Minifigures 3

Hufflepuff crest for Professor Sprout

Cauldron piece doubles as Mandrake pot

Fainted Neville

Large-rimmed glasses

Scarf is attached to hair piece

Layers of long, floaty clothing

Cup for reading tea leaves

DIVINATION

High in the Astronomy Tower, Sybill Trelawney pursues the noble art of Divination. Those who possess the second sight can cast themselves into the beyond and read future events—"the truth lies like a sentence deep within a book waiting to be read." However, some wizards and witches write off the whole subject as hogwash.

SECOND VIEW

Trelawney's minifigure with a leg piece has two sides to her head. The other looks zoned-out, like she's revealing a prophecy.

▲ PROFESSOR TRELAWNEY

Sybill Trelawney is a Seer, which means she can predict the future. Her skill is much weaker than her great-great grandmother's was, however Sybill has learned tricks over the years to cover her shortcomings. She has actually made genuine prophecies; she just doesn't remember.

Set name *Hogwarts Moment: Divination Class*	
Year 2022	**Number** 76396
Pieces 297	**Minifigures** 3

BRICK FACTS

Every Hogwarts Moments set has a subject-specific book. This tile shows a dog named the Grim—it's an Omen of Death.

▼ FORTUNE-TELLING

Up a circular staircase, the Divination classroom has paraphernalia for reading tea leaves and studying the art of crystal-gazing. Harry tries to reads his tea leaves, and Parvati Patil practices clearing her inner eye to see the future in a crystal ball.

Plush, heavy fabrics decorate classroom

Tan owl piece for stone carving

Stacks of teacups for reading tea leaves

Harry has a [g]o at reading tea leaves

Crystal ball

LIFE AT HOGWARTS

THE SORCERER'S STONE

A legendary substance with astonishing powers, the Sorcerer's Stone can transform any metal into gold and produce the Elixir of Life—a potion that makes the drinker immortal. Voldemort, whose defeated spirit is lacking a physical form, covets the Stone so he can restore his body and power. Now it is at Hogwarts, the Dark Lord uses Professor Quirrell to find it.

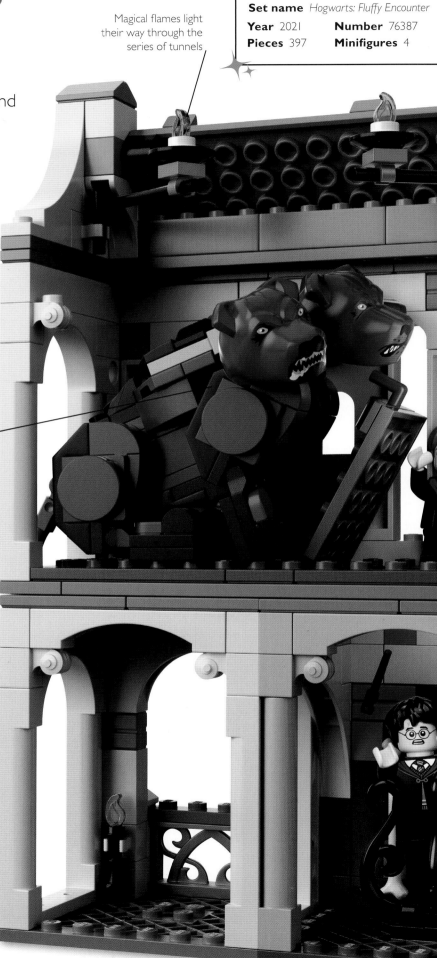

Magical flames light their way through the series of tunnels

Set name	Hogwarts: Fluffy Encounter	
Year 2021	**Number** 76387	
Pieces 397	**Minifigures** 4	

Gryffindor torso design from 2021

From this angle, it looks like the dog is awake—these three eyes are all open

⋀ STONE SEEKER

It's during Harry's first year that the Sorcerer's Stone is moved from Gringotts Wizarding Bank to Hogwarts, so his minifigure has short legs and smart, done-up robes. Realizing that the Stone is at risk, Harry and his friends, Ron and Hermione, race to find it before Voldemort does.

➤ THIRD-FLOOR CORRIDOR

Professor Dumbledore says that the third-floor corridor is strictly out of bounds to all students. This is where the Sorcerer's Stone is hidden, behind a series of magical protections. To stop Voldemort from getting the Stone, Harry, Ron, and Hermione must outwit each obstacle and reach the object before the Dark Lord does.

HERBOLOGIST

Hermione recognizes Devil's Snare and remembers that the way to survive it is to relax. Or failing that, blast it with sunlight.

CHESS WIZARD

Ron loves playing Wizards' Chess. His skills come in handy when his, Harry, and Hermione's lives depend on winning a game of chess.

Harp is enchanted to keep playing

From this angle, it looks like the dog is sleeping—these three eyes are all closed

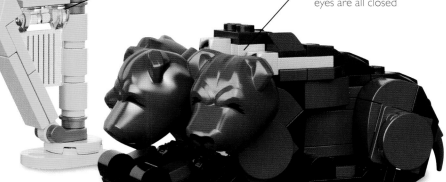

◄ FLUFFY

Fluffy may seem an odd name for a giant dog with three ferocious heads, but Hagrid always sees the best in creatures. Fluffy guards the trapdoor, but there is a secret to getting past him: play some music and he falls into a peaceful sleep.

Brick-built chess pieces can be broken

➤ GAME OF LIFE AND DEATH

The trio faces a giant Wizards' Chessboard and must play their way across the room. The statue pieces can move, their weapons are very real, and losing pieces are smashed to smithereens. Harry takes the empty bishop's square, Hermione is queen-side bishop, and Ron plays as a knight and directs the game.

Magical flames light the board

Quirrell's turban hides Voldemort's face

Devils Snare right under the trapdoor

Panel fits into the LEGO build of the Mirror of Erised

Set name	*Hogwarts Wizard's Chess*	
Year 2021	**Number** 76392	
Pieces 876	**Minifigures** 4	

◄ THE FINAL HURDLE

Professor Quirrell, who is controlled by Voldemort, sees what he desires in the Mirror of Erised—himself holding the Stone—but how does it get it? This hiding place is one of Dumbledore's more brilliant ideas—only someone who doesn't want to use the Stone can retrieve it from the mirror.

POLYJUICE POTION

Have you ever wondered what it would be like to look like someone else? With Polyjuice Potion, you can do just that. Properly prepared, it allows the drinker to temporarily transform him or herself into the physical form of another. However, it's notoriously difficult to make—even Hermoine has never seen a more complicated potion.

◄ POTENT ELIXIR

The ingredients for Polyjuice Potion are Fluxweed (picked on a full moon), Knotgrass, Lacewing Flies, Leeches, powdered Bicorn Horn, shredded Boomslang Skin, and, finally, a piece of the person to be impersonated, such as a hair or toenail. Drink up and try not to be sick!

Transparent 1×1 round plates create liquid effect

Set name	*Hogwarts: Polyjuice Potion Mistake*	
Year 2021		**Number** 76386
Pieces 217		**Minifigures** 4

Second-floor girls' bathroom is rarely used

Central sink lifts up to reveal entrance to Chamber of Secrets

Modular room can be combined with other Hogwarts sets

▲ COOKING UP A PLAN

Hermione has a theory that Draco Malfoy is responsible for opening the Chamber of Secrets. Even though it breaks about 50 school rules, she brews some Polyjuice Potion so she, Ron, and Harry can impersonate Draco's friends —then he'll tell them anything.

Potion must brew in cauldron for a month

Ingredients stolen from school stores

⌃ HARRY/GOYLE

A Harry minifigure in Slytherin robes is an unexpected sight, but swap his hair piece and turn around his head, and Gregory Goyle's face completes the potion's illusion. With the real Crabbe and Goyle dozing with a sleeping draught, all is set. Harry just needs to remember to take off his glasses.

Slytherin robes "borrowed" from Goyle

⌄ RON/CRABBE

Ron's minifigure transforms into Draco's sidekick Vincent Crabbe, while Harry is his other brutish crony, Gregory Goyle. The Slytherin-robed minifigure comes with two hair pieces and a head with two printed sides: Ron's grimace and Crabbe's cake-munching face.

Expression shows how disgusting Crabbe's potion tastes

LEGO piece fits over the minifigure head like a hair piece

⌃ CAT-ASTROPHE

Hermione plucked a hair from Millicent Bulstrode's Slytherin robes, but it turns out not to be hers... Polyjuice Potion is only designed for human transformations, and the hair belonged to Millicent's pet cat! Hermione's furry face is purrfectly cute but takes a while to wear off.

Alternative face print is Mafalda Hopkirks

Water marks from an indoor-rain problem

MASTER OF DISGUISE

In Hogwarts Moment: Defense Against the Dark Arts Class (set 76397), Mad-Eye Moody looks like Barty Crouch Junior. That's because Barty's Polyjuice Potion is wearing off. The Death Eater needs another swig from his hip flask to continue his guise and get close to Harry Potter, while the real Moody is trapped, locked in a magical trunk.

⌃ MINISTRY INTRUDERS

In Hermione and Ron's quest to retrieve Slytherin's locket from Dolores Umbridge, they need to sneak into the Ministry of Magic. They pose as Ministry workers Mafalda Hopkirk and Reg Cattermole and pass unnoticed in The Ministry of Magic (set 76403), until their Polyjuice Potion starts to wear off...

Snake motif first designed for LEGO® NINJAGO®

Transparent Slytherin green

THE CHAMBER OF SECRETS

Many years ago, one of Hogwarts' founders, Salazar Slytherin, fell out with the others over which students the school should admit. He didn't want Hogwarts to teach Muggle-born wizards and witches. The disagreement led Salazar to leave the school. His parting "gift" was a secret room that, legend has it, contains a terrible monster that will rid the school of all who are Muggle-born.

▲ SECRET VAULT

According to legend, the magically sealed Chamber of Secrets can be opened only by the true Heir of Slytherin. The round metal door and serpentine decorations give a clue to the monster inside: a giant snake who travels through the school's pipes. One look in the Basilisk's eyes is fatal.

➤ UPSTAIRS, DOWNSTAIRS

Ordinary school life has been taking place, while all the time, the Chamber of Secrets lurks underneath. Meals are eaten in the Great Hall, lessons are taught in the Defense Against the Dark Arts classroom, and fan mail is answered in Lockhart's office, with no one aware of what lies beneath.

Set name	*Hogwarts Chamber of Secrets*	
Year 2021	**Number** 76389	
Pieces 1,176	**Minifigures** 11	

Telescope for Astronomy lessons

An escaped Chocolate Frog

Small chessboard

School banner conceals the Sorting Hat

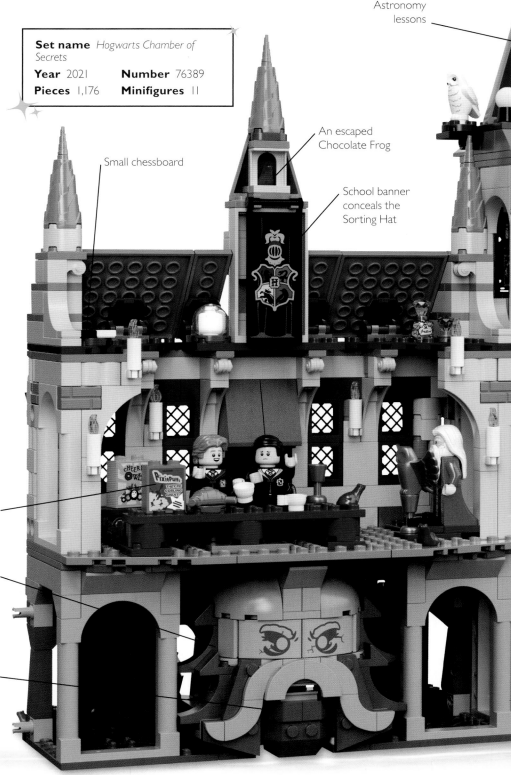

Breakfast cereals include Cheery Owls and Pixie Puffs

Carving of Salazar Slytherin's head

Mouth opens, creating tunnel for Basilisk

BRICK FACTS

Two serpent sentries flank Salazar Slytherin's statue in the Chamber. Their head pieces were first created in gold for the LEGO NINJAGO theme.

Hinged sink panel reveals tunnel

Style of Slytherin robes 50 years ago

➤ THE HEIR OF SLYTHERIN

Fifty years ago, Tom Riddle opened the Chamber of Secrets, and a Muggle-born student was killed. Like Salazar, Tom is in Slytherin House, he's a Parselmouth (he can speak with snakes), and he seeks to get rid of Muggle-born witches and wizards.

▲ ANCIENT PLUMBING

Not many people go in the girls' bathroom on the second floor because it's haunted by Moaning Myrtle. Another reason it might seem creepy is because it conceals the secret entranceway to the Chamber of Secrets—as Harry and his friends discover.

PULLING STRINGS

Tom Riddle's spirit survives in his diary for 50 years, until Ginny Weasley unwittingly unleashes it and reopens the Chamber. After several people (and a cat) are Petrified by the Basilisk, Ginny is taken into the Chamber. Tom (now Voldemort) wants to lure Harry into a trap.

Lockhart's own portraits fill his office walls

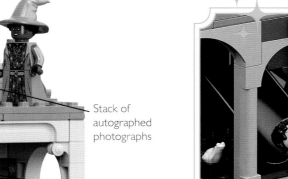

Stack of autographed photographs

Large portrait with two Professor Lockharts

SLIPPERY SLOPE

Placing Hogwarts: Polyjuice Potion Mistake (set 76386) on top of this set, joins the entrance with the tunnel. Harry tumbles down the slide—used in parks in other LEGO sets—in a bid to find and rescue Ginny.

Articulated body pieces

The Sorting Hat

Sword of Gryffindor

▲ A HELPING HAND

Help will always be given at Hogwarts to those who ask for it: Harry is sent invaluable reinforcements from Dumbledore's Office. Fawkes the Phoenix blinds the Basilisk's eyes and delivers the Sorting Hat. The Hat contains the Sword of Gryffindor—just what Harry needs to defeat the giant serpent.

Discarded bones

Poster in Hogsmeade village

SIRIUS BLACK

Harry's third year begins amid alarming rumors of an escaped criminal. The word on Diagon Alley is that the fearsome Siruis Black (who is Harry's godfather!) is guilty of terrible crimes in the name of Voldemort, including betraying Harry's parents. But, don't believe everything you hear. Everything is not quite what it seems!

⌃ IN THE FRAME

Sirius Black's face is framed in wanted posters, plastered across Hogsmeade and beyond by the Ministry of Magic. The wizard was also framed by a friend who set him up for the crimes he was convicted for. Sirius is innocent!

Prison tattoos

JAIL-BREAKER

Fresh from the putrid cells of Azkaban, Sirius is still in his prison-issue garb. He's desperate to clear his name and get revenge on the wizard who set him up.

Unkempt printed beard

ON THE RUN

Sirius's minifigure still hasn't had the chance to clean up or get out of his prison clothes. He's lost his warm overcoat and has gained some rips.

◀ TRAPPED!

Two ghastly Dementor minifigures, sent by the Ministry of Magic to round up the escapee, swoop down on a drained Sirius. Harry tries to keep the deadly envoys at bay with the Patronus Charm, but he's only ever done it in the classroom before.

Set name	*Expecto Patronum*	
Year 2019	**Number** 75945	
Pieces 121	**Minifigures** 4	

Dementor's senses locate by emotion

Weak *Expecto Patronum* charm

Shore of the Black Lake

Stag Patronus sent by a mysterious savior

CAUGHT!

Sirius is saved from the terrible Dementor's kiss at the lake's shore, but he is put in a cell at Hogwarts to await transfer back to Azkaban. Harry and his friends are the only ones who believe in his innocence.

TIME-TURNING

Hermione is a stickler for school rules, but she will bend the rules of time in order to correct injustice. She's been using a magical Time-Turner to attend extra lessons all year. Now she and Harry can go back a couple of hours to right the Ministry's wrongs.

BRICK FACTS

Hermione's minifigure holds a 1x1 printed tile Time-Turner in Hogwarts Hospital Wing (set 76398). In Hagrid's Hut: Buckbeak's Rescue (set 75947), it's printed on her torso.

Set name *Hogwarts Courtyard: Sirius's Rescue*

Year *2022*

Number *76401*

Pieces *345*

Minifigures 3

➤ TO THE RESCUE

Sirius escapes again, but as the Ministry's most wanted wizard, he is still on the run. Life in hiding isn't much fun, especially for someone as lively, sociable, and spirited as Sirius Black. It's a miserable and frustrating existence, but at least Harry can finally get to know his godfather.

Hogwarts tower with makeshift prison cell

Wings and head of an eagle attach to the body of a horse

Time-Turner enables time travel

Seated minifigure attaches to 2x2 brick

Wings clip onto removable brick

◢ HIPPOGRIFF HELPER

With Buckbeak the Hippogriff sentenced to death by the Ministry of Magic and Sirius back in custody, two innocent lives need saving. Harry and Hermione travel back in time to rescue Buckbeak and then he flies Sirius away to safety.

THE TRIWIZARD TOURNAMENT

The ancient Triwizard Tournament is a grueling test for young wizards and witches. Students are selected to be champions, normally one from each of three European schools: Hogwarts, Beauxbatons Academy of Magic, and the Durmstrang Institute. They compete in three difficult and dangerous tasks to see who will be the ultimate Triwizard champion.

THE GOBLET OF FIRE

In Hogwarts Clock Tower (set 75948), Triwizard champion Cedric Diggory enters the ball, passing the Goblet of Fire and its blue flames. This magical object selects who will compete in the Triwizard Tournament. Once chosen, contestants are bound by a magical contract and must take part.

⋁ THE FIRST CHALLENGE

For the first task, each champion must retrieve a golden egg that is being guarded by a huge, ferocious dragon. Perhaps the hardest part is the waiting beforehand. At least the champions have their own tent where they can rest and prepare. Inside the shared tent are refreshments, a bed, and drawers for storing belongings.

One wall is decorated with the Durmstrang and Beauxbatons school crests

Hogwarts school crest

LEGO® Technic axle with a tow ball holds wings in place

Viktor Krum waits for his turn to face a dragon

Much-needed refreshments

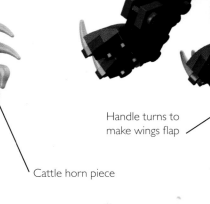

Handle turns to make wings flap

Cattle horn piece

Set name
Hungarian Horntail Triwizard Challenge
Year 2019
Number 75946
Pieces 265
Minifigures 4

➤ HUNGARIAN HORNTAIL

Harry draws the short straw when he selects the Hungarian Horntail—it's a particularly vicious dragon. For their turns, Viktor faces a Chinese Fireball dragon; Fleur a Welsh Green; and Cedric selects a Swedish Short-snout.

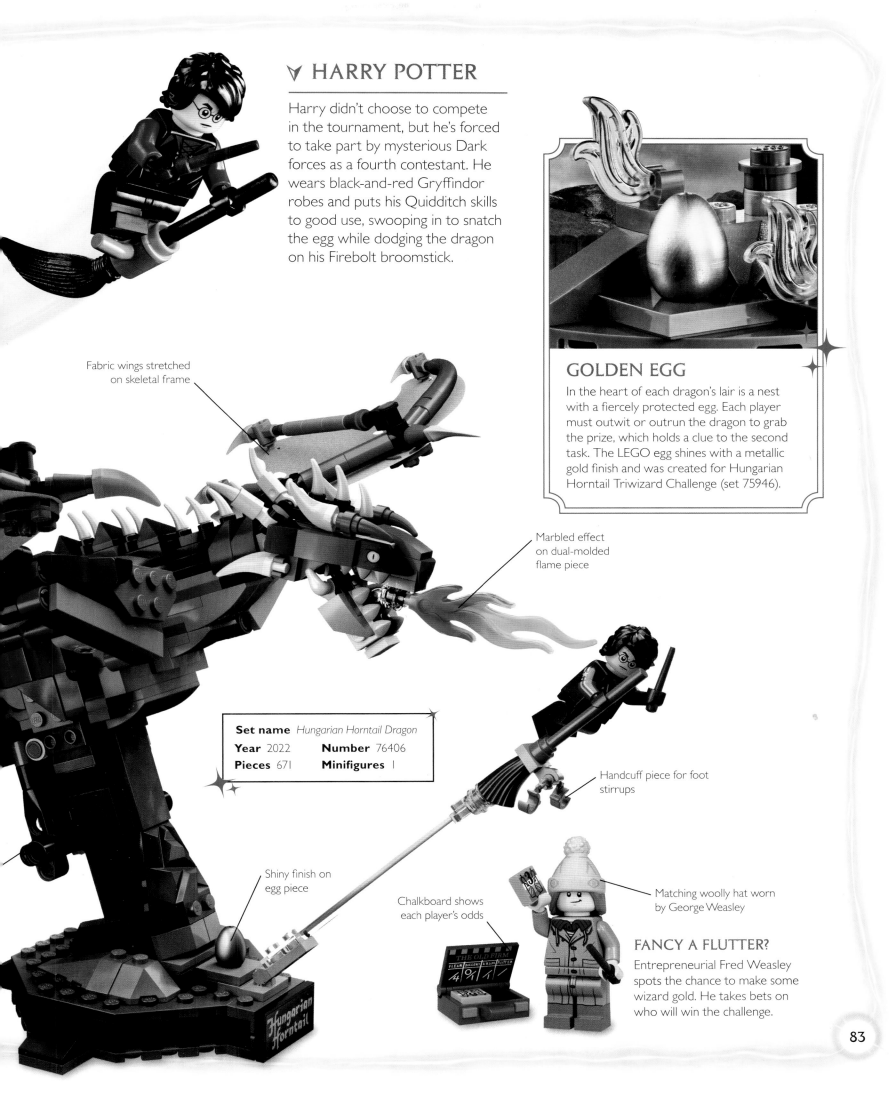

⍌ HARRY POTTER

Harry didn't choose to compete in the tournament, but he's forced to take part by mysterious Dark forces as a fourth contestant. He wears black-and-red Gryffindor robes and puts his Quidditch skills to good use, swooping in to snatch the egg while dodging the dragon on his Firebolt broomstick.

GOLDEN EGG

In the heart of each dragon's lair is a nest with a fiercely protected egg. Each player must outwit or outrun the dragon to grab the prize, which holds a clue to the second task. The LEGO egg shines with a metallic gold finish and was created for Hungarian Horntail Triwizard Challenge (set 75946).

Fabric wings stretched on skeletal frame

Marbled effect on dual-molded flame piece

Set name	*Hungarian Horntail Dragon*	
Year 2022	**Number** 76406	
Pieces 671	**Minifigures** 1	

Handcuff piece for foot stirrups

Shiny finish on egg piece

Chalkboard shows each player's odds

Matching woolly hat worn by George Weasley

FANCY A FLUTTER?

Entrepreneurial Fred Weasley spots the chance to make some wizard gold. He takes bets on who will win the challenge.

TRIWIZARD CONTESTANTS

Traditionally, three champions compete against each other in the Triwizard Tournament. The champions are their school's best examples of courage, strength, and magical skill. However, this year Harry Potter was mysteriously selected by the Goblet of Fire as a fourth champion, along with a student from each of the three schools.

HUFFLEPUFF HERO

Cedric tackles the first Tournament task in long yellow-and-black Hufflepuff robes. He wears thick gray gloves to grab the golden egg guarded by a savage Swedish Short-Snout dragon. He uses Transfiguration to distract the dragon and gets away by the skin of his teeth.

Handles can be gripped by minifigure

Logo represents all four Hogwarts houses

Double yellow stripe printed on sides of legs

◀ CEDRIC DIGGORY

The original Hogwarts champion, Cedric is a very popular student. He's in the sixth year and has succeeded both in the classroom and out of it. He has been a prefect, as well as a captain and a Seeker of the Hufflepuff Quidditch team. Dressed in Hufflepuff colors, with his surname printed on the back of his torso, this Cedric minifigure is raring to go.

DAPPER DIGGORY

The tournament isn't all just hard work for the champions. Cedric Diggory scrubs up well for the Yule Ball. His minifigure has his usual swept-back hair piece and wears a very smart black dinner jacket and tie with a dress shirt.

Chinese-inspired cheongsam-style dress

CHO CHANG

Cedric invites Cho Chang to be his partner at the Yule Ball. She appears in her formal dress robes in the 2020 Advent Calendar (set 75981).

BRICK FACTS

The glittering Triwizard Cup is so grand that it stands almost as tall as a minifigure, though it can still be held aloft with a single hand. It is one piece and has metallic printing around the rim.

Short, dark, textured hair piece

Durmstrang crest with double-headed eagle and stag's head

VALIANT VIKTOR

Viktor's double-sided head can turn around to enjoy the Yule Ball festivities. Now smiling, he looks gallant in a red military-style jacket. Leather straps across his torso hold a fur-lined cape over one shoulder. His belt buckle has a miniature version of the Durmstrang crest.

2x1 brick and tile for skirt

HERMIONE GRANGER

Everyone is curious to know who the poster-boy Viktor will ask to the Yule Ball. The answer is Hermione, who looks stunning in pink ruffles.

◢ VIKTOR KRUM

The Goblet of Fire selects Viktor Krum from the Durmstrang Institute. He's met with great excitement at Hogwarts because he's already famous as the Seeker on the Bulgarian National Quidditch team. The Viktor minifigure has two expressions. His furrowed brow here suggests he is focused on outwitting his dragon, a Chinese Fireball.

Quilted tunic

Long hair tied up for challenge

Fleur's initials

◀ FLEUR DELACOUR

The brightest and the best from Beauxbatons Academy of Magic, Fleur Delacour is a very skilled witch, particularly with charms. Fleur defeats her Common Welsh Green dragon by enchanting it to sleep. Her minifigure wears a blue-and-gold tracksuit with a Beauxbatons crest on the back.

FANCY FLEUR

Fleur swaps her practical legs piece for an elegant sloped skirt brick for the Yule Ball. She wears an evening dress of silver-gray satin with leaf details. Fleur is so dazzling because her grandmother was a Veela—a semi-human, enchantingly beautiful creature.

Hogwarts crest

GRYFFINDOR VIP

Harry has stylish dress robes for the Yule Ball. His minifigure wears a classic dinner-style jacket with a white dress shirt and white bow tie in the 2020 Advent Calendar (set 75981), seen here with a festive fireplace, and in Hogwarts Clock Tower (set 75948).

Dual-molded arms with yellow printing

➤ HARRY POTTER

Compared to the other contestants, Harry is at an age disadvantage because he's only a fourth-year. His minifigure's shorter legs are in the newer medium-size piece rather than the standard height. One side of his face looks concerned about facing a dragon, but the other has a quietly confident smile.

BEAUXBATONS' CARRIAGE

Hogwarts cannot be found on a map, there's no direct road, and witches and wizards can't Apparate in its grounds, so visitors often find their own clever ways to get there. When the Beauxbatons Academy of Magic students arrive for the Triwizard Tournament, they make a stylish appearance in a flying coach pulled by elegant, white horses.

➤ FLEUR DELACOUR

A future Triwizard champion, Fleur arrives at Hogwarts in the carriage. She hasn't been selected for the Tournament yet, so she wears the same blue Beauxbatons uniform as her classmates. Fleur's hair and hat are a single piece and the other side of her double-printed head shows her singing.

Hair is tied back in a low ponytail

Full-sized legs are molded in two shades of blue

A WARM WELCOME

Groundskeeper Hagrid guides the carriage in to land. He greets the new guests and helps them unload their luggage. Hagrid also gives the Abraxan horses a well-deserved drink from the bottle in the trunk—they only drink the finest whiskey!

Moveable head with printed reins

Cape is printed on the front and back of torso

◄ GABRIELLE DELACOUR

Fleur's little sister, Gabrielle, shares the same torso and hair piece as Fleur, but has shorter legs and freckles on her face. The other side of Gabrielle's head shows her sleeping. She is put in an enchanted sleep at the bottom of the Great Lake to be rescued by Fleur as part of the tournament's second task.

Fur collar

Extra-tall skirt piece is printed on the front and the back

➤ MADAME MAXIME

The half-giant Headmistress of Beauxbatons, Olympe Maxime, accompanies her students. Her minifigure is even taller than Hagrid's thanks to a sloped skirt that is bigger than regular skirt pieces by the height of a standard LEGO brick.

BRICK FACTS

After the journey, it's time for tea! This teapot appears in six other LEGO Harry Potter sets, including for reading tea leaves in Hogwarts Moment: Divination Class (set 76396).

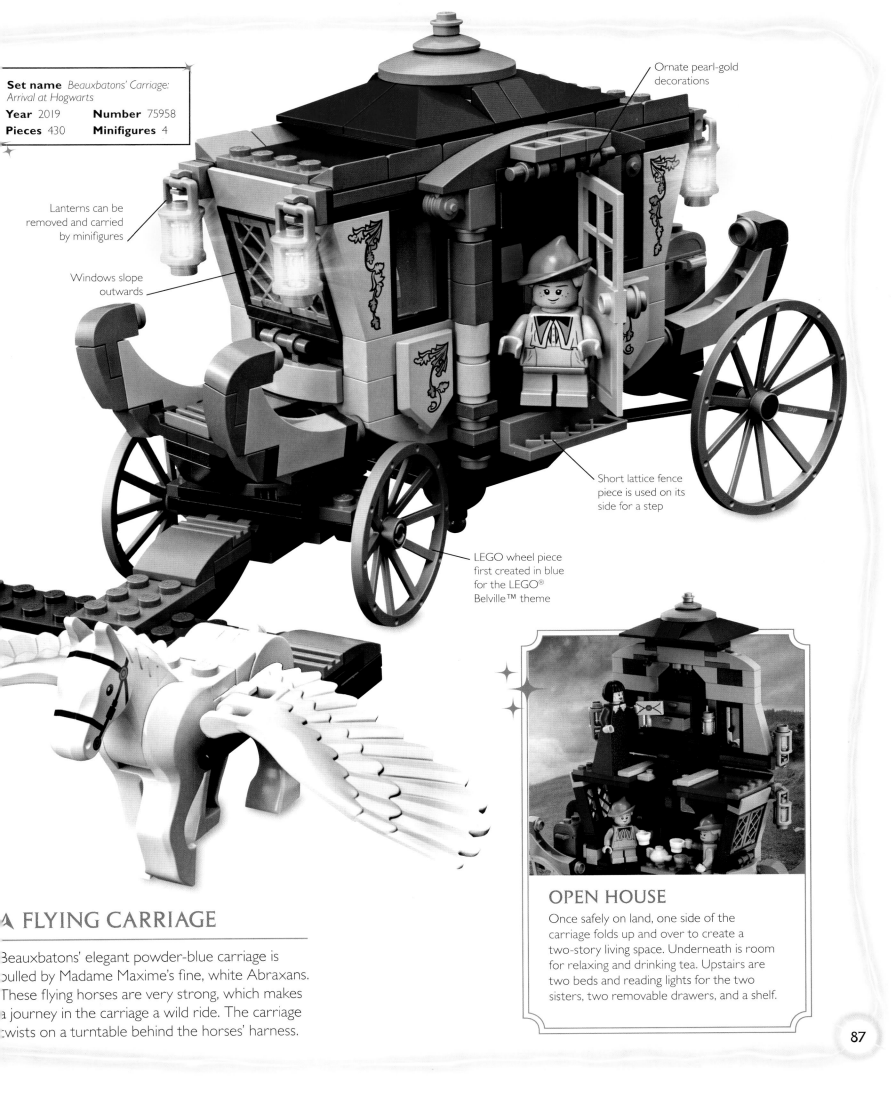

Set name *Beauxbatons' Carriage: Arrival at Hogwarts*

Year 2019   **Number** 75958
Pieces 430   **Minifigures** 4

Ornate pearl-gold decorations

Lanterns can be removed and carried by minifigures

Windows slope outwards

Short lattice fence piece is used on its side for a step

LEGO wheel piece first created in blue for the LEGO® Belville™ theme

◢ FLYING CARRIAGE

Beauxbatons' elegant powder-blue carriage is pulled by Madame Maxime's fine, white Abraxans. These flying horses are very strong, which makes a journey in the carriage a wild ride. The carriage twists on a turntable behind the horses' harness.

OPEN HOUSE

Once safely on land, one side of the carriage folds up and over to create a two-story living space. Underneath is room for relaxing and drinking tea. Upstairs are two beds and reading lights for the two sisters, two removable drawers, and a shelf.

THE YULE BALL

The tradition of the Yule Ball is as old as the Triwizard Tournament itself. The grand event celebrates international friendship between the three schools and gives the champions a break from the grueling Tournament. On Christmas Eve night, everyone can dance their troubles away. Hogwarts Clock Tower (set 75948) sets the stage and is decorated as a winter wonderland for the festivities.

CHRISTMAS COUNTDOWN

Along with the Triwizard Tournament, the Yule Ball festivities are a focus of the 2020 Advent Calendar (set 75981). Harry holds a 2×3 tile printed as the poster for the ball that reveals a performance by the Weird Sisters.

WINTER WONDERLAND

Icicle-encrusted tables, sparkling glassware, and elegant ice sculptures adorn the busy ballroom. The buildable ice sculptures are made from transparent, pointed pieces. Minifigures of Dumbledore and Madame Maxime pause to chat, wearing their finest dress robes. Ron is talking to Fleur —perhaps he'll ask her to dance?

➤ CASTLE AT CHRISTMAS

The festive Clock Tower set can be joined with other LEGO Hogwarts Castle sets to make a larger scene. It includes a three-story tower, the entrance hall, the Defense Against the Dark Arts classroom, the hospital wing with two beds, the prefects' bathroom, Dumbledore's office, and a star-topped Christmas tree.

Minifigure's ski pole piece

Upper tower holds Dumbledore's office

Set name	Hogwarts Clock Tower	
Year 2019		**Number** 75948
Pieces 922		**Minifigures** 8

Ron feels out of place in his unfashionable dress robes

Transparent ice sculpture

Icicle is a unicorn horn piece

Cones molded
with roof tiles

Dupatta (scarf) crosses torso

Choli (blouse)

PARVATI PATIL

The Patil twins wear chaniya-choli or ghagra-choli formal dress inspired by their Indian heritage. Parvati dresses up for the ball and goes with Harry.

PADMA PATIL

The sisters' outfits match but are in opposite color combinations of bright pink and salmon. Padma wears hers to the ball with a very grumpy Ron.

Inverse transparent radar dish for larger clock face

Tree from Hogwarts' grounds

REVOLVING DANCE FLOOR

The Ball is first and foremost a dance so all students have dance lessons beforehand. The four champions and their partners open the dance, including Viktor Krum with Hermione. A revolving dance floor function really gets the minifigures moving by spinning them in two directions simultaneously.

Madame Maxime wears an elegant wrap dress

THE BLACK LAKE

The golden egg that Harry retrieved during the first challenge of the Triwizard Tournament reveals a clue about the second task. It says, "Come seek us where our voices sound, we cannot sing above the ground, an hour long you'll have to look, to recover what we took." The competition takes place in Hogwarts' grounds at, or rather in, the Black Lake.

Clock counts down one hour

Set name
Triwizard Tournament: The Black Lake
Year 2023
Number 76420
Pieces 349
Minifigures 5

Tower stands in the middle of the lake

➤ SPECTATOR TOWER

All four contestants—Harry, Cedric, Viktor, and Fleur—begin on the tower built out on the lake. They jump down into the water and their hour begins. Each has found a different way to breathe underwater. They must find precious items as well as fight off water demon Grindylows.

Rowing bo
ready for
emergenc
rescues

Pearlescent Grindylow element

LEGO ingot pieces for old, water-worn stone

Water-swept hair

◄ STOLEN TREASURE

The night before the trial a treasure of sorts was taken from each of the contestants and placed at the bottom of the Black Lake. Harr is supposed to rescue Ron, and Hermione is for Viktor Krum to retrieve. They are kept in an enchanted sleep and protected by Merpeople in one of their villages.

Alternative face is awake

Sea-grass piece appears in more than 20 LEGO sets

Chains are secured to an archway built by Merpeople

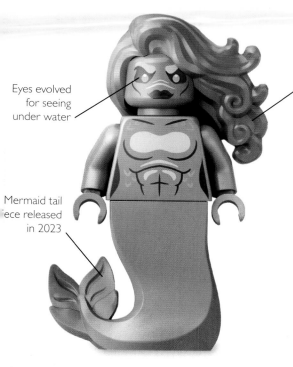

Eyes evolved for seeing under water

Long hair wafts with the sway of the water

Mermaid tail piece released in 2023

➤ AQUATIC HARRY

Harry gets a tip from his Herbologist friend Neville: Gillyweed. The edible plant takes effect quickly, forging breathing gills in his neck so he can breathe underwater. It also webs his hands and extends his feet with webbed flippers to help him swim faster.

Printed gills for breathing under water

Simplified Hogwarts emblem on Gryffindor red

Flipper pieces the color of Harry's skin

⋀ MERPERSON

Merpeople are found all over the world, but there's a colony in Hogwarts' backyard living in the Black Lake. The Merpeople look fierce, but they're helping Professor Dumbledore with the tournament.

Shark head has a fin attached to its back

GILLYWEED

You can find a bottle of this rare weed in Hogwarts Icons—Collectors' Edition (set 76391). LEGO vine pieces fill a transparent brick-built stoppered bottle.

➤ VIKTOR THE SHARK

There's something fishy about Bulgarian Bon-Bon Viktor Krum. He meets the challenge of the task by transfiguring his head into a shark's. He can breathe underwater, scent his target, and use his sharp teeth to cut Hermione's bindings.

Durmstrang school logo

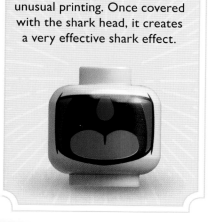
Bubble gives a constant supply of fresh oxygen

➤ NAUTICAL CEDRIC

Cedric Diggory casts a Bubble-Head Charm. It creates a protective bubble around his nose and mouth so he can breathe under water for the duration of the Black Lake task. Fleur Delacour also uses a Bubble-head charm, but she's thwarted in the competition by a Grindylow attack.

Waterproof wrist watch

LORD VOLDEMORT

Watch out! This striking minifigure is Lord Voldemort—the vilest Dark wizard ever known. He was once a Hogwarts schoolboy, but now people are so afraid of him that they do not even dare speak his name. They call him only He Who Must Not Be Named or the Dark Lord. Voldemort craves power and will destroy anyone who stands in his way.

Flat nose with snakelike nostrils

Wand casts Dark curses and spells

Green trim on black robes

Curved sloped brick for long, wizard robes

⌃ THE DARK LORD

Voldemort was defeated many years ago, but not completely destroyed. A piece of his soul survived and waited years to regain a physical form. Now Voldemort has a body again, he is growing in strength and has solid LEGO minifigures. They show his pale face with bloodshot eyes and a flat nose like a snake's.

Bone-white skin

Nagini clips into Voldemort's hand

◂ HEIR OF SLYTHERIN

Like his distant ancestor Salazar Slytherin, Voldemort is a Parselmouth, which means he can talk to snakes. Fittingly, his companion in the LEGO Harry Potter Series 1 (71022) is his large snake named Nagini. Voldemort wears long Slytherin-green robes.

HAPLESS HOST

Professor Quirinus Quirrell's minifigure reveals an appalling secret: he is sharing his body with Voldemort! Not only is Quirrell unable to defeat his own parasite, but he brings it into Hogwarts. Hidden underneath Quirrell's lavender turban lies his master's withered, scowling face.

Forked tongue

BAH HUMBUG

For the 2022 Advent Calendar (set 76404), Voldemort flashes some festive red by sticking out his brightly colored snakelike, forked tongue.

Muddy robes from battle

BATTLE-READY

Perhaps The Battle of Hogwarts (set 76415) is taking its toll on Voldemort's drained face—but then, he always looks like that.

TOM RIDDLE

It's hard to believe that 50 years ago, the Dark Lord was a Slytherin boy called Tom Marvolo Riddle. During Harry's second year, Tom emerges from a diary and reopens the Chamber of Secrets, releasing the Basilisk. His exclusive LEGO minifigure came with DK's LEGO *Harry Potter Magical Treasury*.

Old-fashioned Slytherin uniform

Mold was used in 2016 for a minifigure baby in a tan papoose

BRICK FACTS

The Rise of Voldemort (set 75965), includes the Deathly Hallows symbol. Voldemort is seeking the Elder Wand (|), the Resurrection Stone (O), and the Invisibility Cloak (△). Legend says they can conquer death.

⌃ SMALL, BUT DANGEROUS

This small LEGO piece may look like a bizarre baby, but it is the Dark Lord! Reduced to just a fragment of his soul, Voldemort existed only as a tiny, weak creature. He has been plotting to get a proper body and finally in the Little Hangleton graveyard, he is close to achieving it.

Set name *The Rise of Voldemort*	
Year 2019	**Number** 75965
Pieces 184	**Minifigures** 5

⯈ THE RISE OF VOLDEMORT

In this graveyard in Little Hangleton, Voldemort literally rises from beneath the ground with a new physical body thanks to a LEGO flipping mechanism. A cauldron holds a potion that brings the Dark Lord back in a strong, human form. Held prisoner, Harry's minifigure can only watch on helplessly.

Gravestone reads "Tom Riddle"

Moveable scythe holds Harry in place

Cauldron brews potion for bringing Voldemort back to full strength

Gray stone frog decorates gravestone

Flipping section lifts Voldemort's figure out of the bare ground

VOLDEMORT'S FOLLOWERS

Voldemort is one of the most powerful wizards ever known, but even he can't do everything alone. He has an army of obliging followers. They carry out his orders, sometimes due to loyalty and shared beliefs, but mostly out of plain fear. However, Voldemort gives no loyalty in return. He regards everyone as disposable when they are no longer useful.

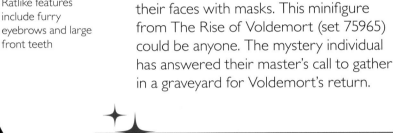

Bent wizard hat does not appear in any other LEGO set

Skull mask is printed on a black head piece

➤ DEATH EATER

Voldemort's most loyal group of supporters are called Death Eaters. To protect their identities, they cover their faces with masks. This minifigure from The Rise of Voldemort (set 75965) could be anyone. The mystery individual has answered their master's call to gather in a graveyard for Voldemort's return.

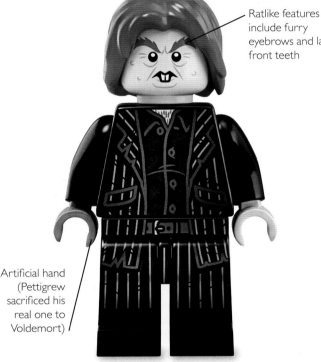

Ratlike features include furry eyebrows and large front teeth

Artificial hand (Pettigrew sacrificed his real one to Voldemort)

SCABBERS

If you smell a rat, it could be Ron's pet, Scabbers. Or it could be because there is deception afoot. Scabbers is actually the Animagus Peter Pettigrew, who has been biding his time, living in hiding with the unknowing Weasley family.

⌃ PETER PETTIGREW

At school, Peter Pettigrew was a great friend of Sirius Black, Remus Lupin, and James Potter (Harry's father). However, he later betrayed them to Voldemort. Everyone thought he died a long time ago, but he has actually been in hiding. Pettigrew is a rat Animagus, which means he can transform into that animal at will.

Hair piece has a low ponytail at the back

Ministry of Magic tie pin

◄ CORBAN YAXLEY

A long-serving Death Eater, Corban Yaxley believes in the superiority of pure-blooded wizards. After Voldemort seizes control of the Ministry of Magic, Yaxley is given the influential role of Head of the Department of Magical Law Enforcement, which gives him terrible power over the fate of Muggle-borns.

Golden pocket watch

Wild, curly hair

Stitched leather corset

BEHIND BARS

Handcuffed and in filthy prison robes, Bellatrix's minifigure from the LEGO Harry Potter Series 2 (set 71028) is serving time in Azkaban for her terrible crimes during the First Wizarding War. However, she's soon free after a mass break-out of the most vicious witches and wizards.

◄ BELLATRIX LESTRANGE

Devoted to Lord Voldemort, Bellatrix is the Dark Lord's right-hand woman and an expert dueler. This menacing minifigure has no mercy and cackles with heartless glee at others' suffering. Proud to be called Voldemort's most faithful servant, she even sacrifices her own family for him.

Large eyes have no pupils

Scarred torso

► SCABIOR

cabior is a callous wizard. He doesn't ollow the Dark Lord directly but is very appy to work as a Snatcher in exchange r wizard gold. He captures those who ppose Voldemort and delivers them the Dark Lord, partly to line his own ockets, or it could be because he enjoys eing cruel.

Single black glove

Alternative face print is scared

Pink scarf belonged to Hermione

▲ FENRIR GREYBACK

If you're bitten by Fenrir Greyback, you don't turn into a LEGO minifigure— you turn into a werewolf! The vicious creature joins Voldemort's followers. Creepy Greyback doesn't particularly support the Dark Lord, he just selfishly wants to benefit from the chaos the Death Eaters create.

A ring of fire surrounds the Burrow

◄ THE HEAT OF BATTLE

During the holidays, the Death Eaters' idea of fun is to besiege the Weasley family with fire and curses. In Attack on the Burrow (set 75980), Fenrir Greyback and Bellatrix Lestrange relish wreaking fiery havoc on the Weasley's festivities and damaging the Burrow.

DUMBLEDORE'S ARMY

In Harry's fifth year, Professor Umbridge prevents students from learning any practical defensive skills. However, it's clear to Harry, and those who trust him, that Voldemort is back. They need to be prepared, so a group takes matters into their own wand-wielding hands. If school won't teach them, they'll teach themselves. They name their group Dumbledore's Army.

∨ THE ROOM OF REQUIREMENT

The Room of Requirement is equipped with everything the students need, from a blackboard, plenty of space for practical exercises, and even an alternative exit when Filch is keeping watch outside. Harry teaches them Disarming (*Expelliamus!*), Stunning (*Stupefy!*), Shrinking (*Diminuendo!*), Blasting (*Reducto!*), and the very advanced Patronus Charm (*Expecto Patronum!*)

∨ HIDDEN ENTRANCE

Normally appearing as a plain stone wall, the Room of Requirement—also known as the Come-and-Go Room—appears only when someone has real need of it. It's exactly the space Dumbledore's Army needs—it's like Hogwarts wants them to fight back!

LEGO wall panel slides to reveal doorway

Harsh new school rules decreed by Dolores Umbridge

Set name	*Hogwarts Room of Requirement*	
Year 2020		**Number** 75966
Pieces 193		**Minifigures** 4

Pillars only extend part way so students have lots of room

Hermione's Patronus is an otter

Hare is the Patronus produced by Luna

Original members of the Order of the Phoenix

Cedric Diggory

◄ MASTERMIND

The idea for Dumbledore's Army came from Hermione. She was the one who saw the need and a way to meet it. She was also the one capable of persuading Harry to take on the task of teaching the group. She finds breaking school rules uncharacteristically exciting.

Longer leg piece for fifth-year characters

LUNA LOVEGOOD

Always open to an alternative way of thinking, Luna signs up without hesitation to join the unconventional group.

Messy tie pairs with casual cardigan

► TRUSTED TEACHER

Harry leads the sessions, sharing his experiences, knowledge, and practical tips with his fellow students. If they're going to have any chance of beating Voldemort, they need to know what it's really like to face Voldemort and his Death Eaters.

HANNAH ABBOTT

A Hufflepuff in Harry's year, Hannah is one of many who join Dumbledore's Army. Her minifigure comes with Hogwarts Students Accessories Set (set 40419).

CHO CHANG

Ravenclaw Seeker Cho Chang was very close with Cedric, who was killed by Voldemort. She understands the threat and joins Dumbledore's Army to be ready to fight back.

▼ DEATH EATER DUMMY

The room even provides a life-size mannequin for practicing spells on. Half-minifigure, half-wheeled build, the stand-in Death Eater can be disarmed, stunned, and even shrunk. The wooden construction takes spells but doesn't fight back.

Terrifying face instils fear

Target for aiming practice

Warming fire through the winter months

Small wheel piece with axle is in more than 300 LEGO sets

CHRISTMAS WISHES

Spending time together with the common purpose and focus of Dumbledore's Army, Harry and Cho Chang become close over the fall term. In the last session before Christmas, after everyone else has left the Room of Requirement, they share a kiss under the mistletoe.

THE WIZARDING WORLD

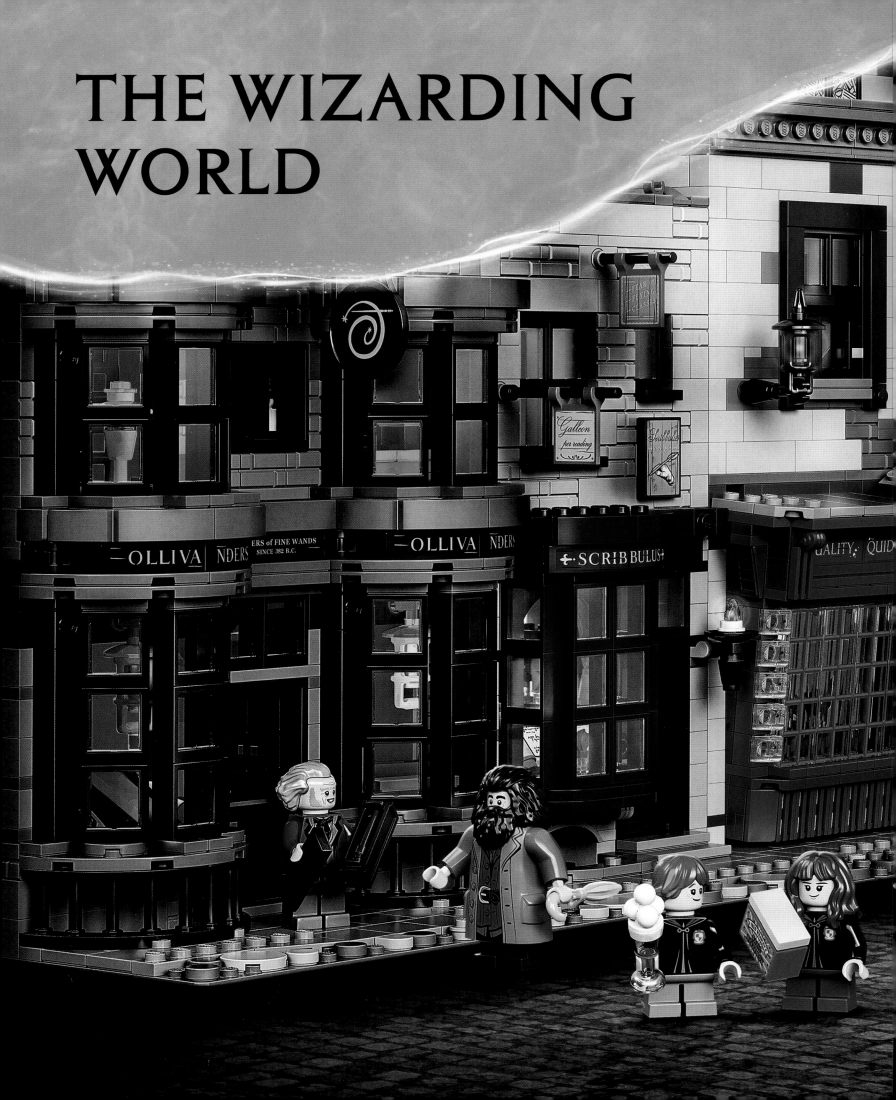

MAGICAL CREATURES

It's not just wizards and witches who are kept hidden from Muggle eyes. There's a whole world of strange and wonderful creatures that would give Muggles a shock. They might recognize the Acromantula from the spiders in their bathrooms (albeit they are on a much bigger scale!), but dragons, centaurs, and Phoenixes are usually thought to be the stuff of legend.

Post and chain stop Buckbeak flying away

Minifigure head piece in orange

Set name *Hagrid's Hut: Buckbeak's Rescue*

Year 2019   **Number** 75947

Pieces 496   **Minifigures** 6

ⅴ BUCKBEAK

Poor Buckbeak is a proud Hippogriff who upset Draco Malfoy and has been sentenced to death. Half-horse and half-eagle, Hippogriffs are very quick to attack if they feel they have been insulted. Buckbeak is now tied up in Hagrid's pumpkin patch, but Hermione has a plan to save him.

Green flower piece is used as pumpkin stem

ⅴ CENTAUR

Centaurs are an ancient species with a proud character. They certainly don't like to be referred to as half-human and half-horse. They're skilled at Divination, Astronomy, and healing. Centaurs shun humans, but Harry and Hermione meet some on a trip into the Forbidden Forest.

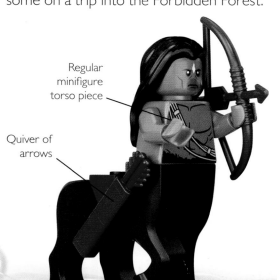

Regular minifigure torso piece

Quiver of arrows

Hand can clip into minifigure's hand

CORNISH PIXIE

Electric blue with impish faces, Cornish Pixies are small in size but big on causing mischief. Their LEGO® mold is cast in bright transparent blue.

FLYING FIENDS

In Hogwarts Chamber of Secrets (set 76389), Professor Lockhart lets loose a cageful of Cornish Pixies in Defense Against the Dark Arts class. They might seem like a mild choice, but the tricky blighters cause chaos and even lift children up by their ears!

➢ OWLS

Owls (not to be confused with OWLs—Ordinary Wizarding Level exams) form close bonds with witches and wizards. As well as being beloved pets, they keep up communication in the wizarding world by delivering post. They can find any recipient, even one who is in hiding.

Owl mold with outstretched wings first created in 2020

The Daily Prophet on regular subscription

OWLERY

As an important hub of communication, Hogwarts has its own Owlery. The owls of students and staff have perches here, and visiting birds can rest after bringing post, before setting off on their return journeys. Students and staff come here to give their owls post, much like visiting the post office.

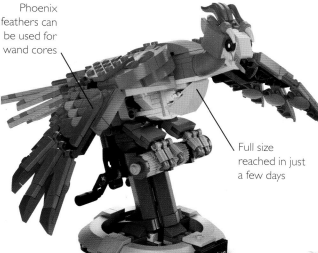

Phoenix feathers can be used for wand cores

Full size reached in just a few days

Set name	*Fawkes, Dumbledore's Phoenix*
Year	2021
Number	76394
Pieces	597
Minifigures	1

⩘ ABRAXANS

A particularly large and powerful breed of flying horse, the majestic Abraxan requires strong handling and drinks only the finest whiskey. Madame Maxime breeds Abraxans and they pull her school's flying carriage.

⩘ FAWKES

The most well-known Phoenix is Fawkes, who lives in Dumbledore's Office at Hogwarts. When a Phoenix reaches old age, he or she bursts into flames and is then reborn from the ashes. The birds are incredibly strong, their tears have healing properties, and their birdsong is very powerful.

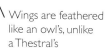

Wings are feathered like an owl's, unlike a Thestral's

Meat for carnivorous Thestral

Wings are leathery like a bat's

◄ THESTRALS

Only those who have seen death can see a Thestral and its distinctive appearance. A breed of winged horse, Thestrals have a glossy coat that stretches over their fleshless, skeletal bodies. A group of Thestrals pull the carriages at Hogwarts.

Apple is rejected by baby Thestral

Eyeless face—Dementors navigate by sensing people's feelings

Mouth ready to steal a soul with a Dementor's Kiss

Raggedy cape

Twisted, smokelike base

DANGEROUS CREATURES

Razor teeth, sharp talons, slathering jaws, plus magical ways of causing harm—there's no shortage of dangers in the wizarding world. Some magical creatures will attack before anyone has time to get their wand out. Perhaps they are hungry or maybe they just attack on instinct. Students should pay attention in Care of Magical Creatures class to recognize the danger signs and be ready with the best defense—even if it's only running away!

▲ DEMENTOR

Ghastly Dementors feed on happiness. These foul floating fiends are used by the Ministry of Magic to guard the wizard prison Azkaban. Those unlucky enough to encounter a Dementor are drained of all hope, peace, and happiness and may even experience the Dementor's Kiss—a fate worse than death.

ON TRACK

On the hunt for escaped convict Sirius Black, Dementors stop the Hogwarts Express. One even boards the train and attacks Harry. Fortunately the new Defense Against the Dark Arts teacher, Professor Lupin, is on hand to dispel it with the Patronus Charm—and give Harry some medicinal chocolate.

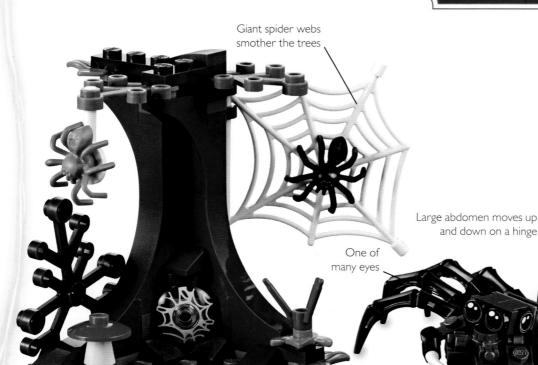

Giant spider webs smother the trees

One of many eyes

Deadly fang

Baby Acromantula

Large abdomen moves up and down on a hinge

Solid leg piece clips to body

▼ ARAGOG

It's the stuff of Ron's nightmares: a monstrous, spiderlike Acromantula that's so huge it can clasp a minifigure in its fearsome jaws. Aragog lives in the Forbidden Forest and calls Hagrid—but no one else—a friend. Aragog appears in LEGO form with a giant web and five baby Acromantulas.

Set name *Aragog's Lair*
Year 2018
Number 75950
Pieces 157
Minifigures 2

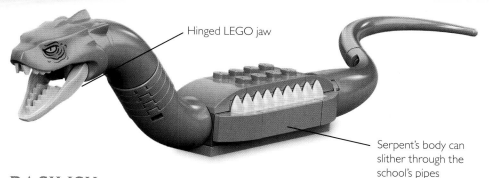

Hinged LEGO jaw

Serpent's body can slither through the school's pipes

⋀ BASILISK

Looking the monstrous snakelike Basilisk in its eyes means instant death—even a reflected glance can cause Petrification. However, its sharp fangs have useful magical properties. During Harry's second year, the Chamber of Secrets is unsealed, revealing a Basilisk dwelling within.

⋁ UKRAINIAN IRONBELLY

There are more species of dragon than you can shake a broomstick at, and the Ukrainian Ironbelly is one of the largest. Harry has to face one at the Gringotts Wizarding Bank.

BRICK FACTS

The large snake called Nagini is Voldemort's constant companion. Her LEGO piece is a single mold that slithers alongside her master or can clip into his minifigure's hand.

Mind has no memory of being human

Curved minifigure legs with paws

⋀ WEREWOLF

Every full moon, afflicted humans become wild, savage werewolves. Werewolf bites are either deadly or pass the terrible condition onto the poor victim. Werewolves tend to live in their own communities, but Remus Lupin manages his condition within wizarding society.

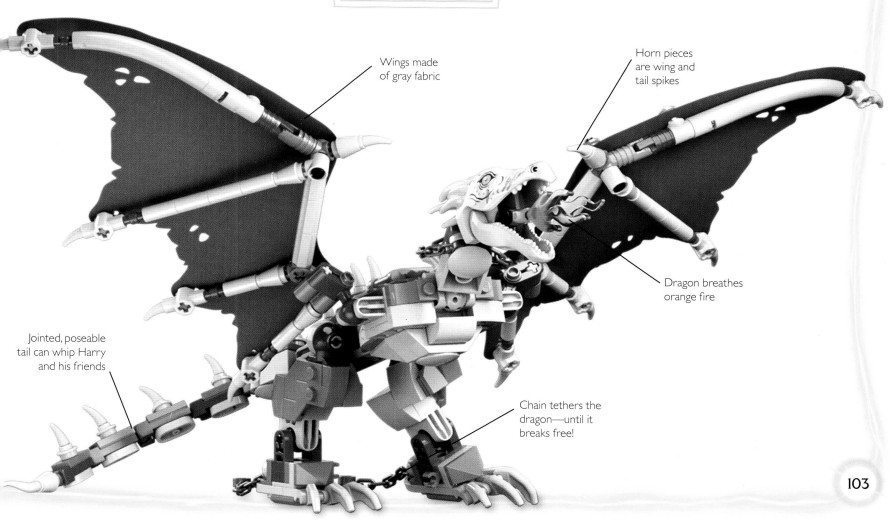

Wings made of gray fabric

Horn pieces are wing and tail spikes

Dragon breathes orange fire

Jointed, poseable tail can whip Harry and his friends

Chain tethers the dragon—until it breaks free!

DIAGON ALLEY

Welcome to Diagon Alley! When witches and wizards want a spot of window shopping or need to stock up on broom-cupboard essentials, this is where they come. Magically shielded from prying Muggle eyes, the famous wizarding shopping street is entered by tapping bricks in the wall of the courtyard of the Leaky Cauldron pub in central London.

▼ SHOPPING STREET

Diagon Alley (set 75978) captures the variety of the cobbled street's crooked, charming architecture with a range of building techniques and variations of rooves, windows, and doors. The street-scene and minifigures relate to shopping trips that Harry makes to prepare for his first, second and sixth years at Hogwarts.

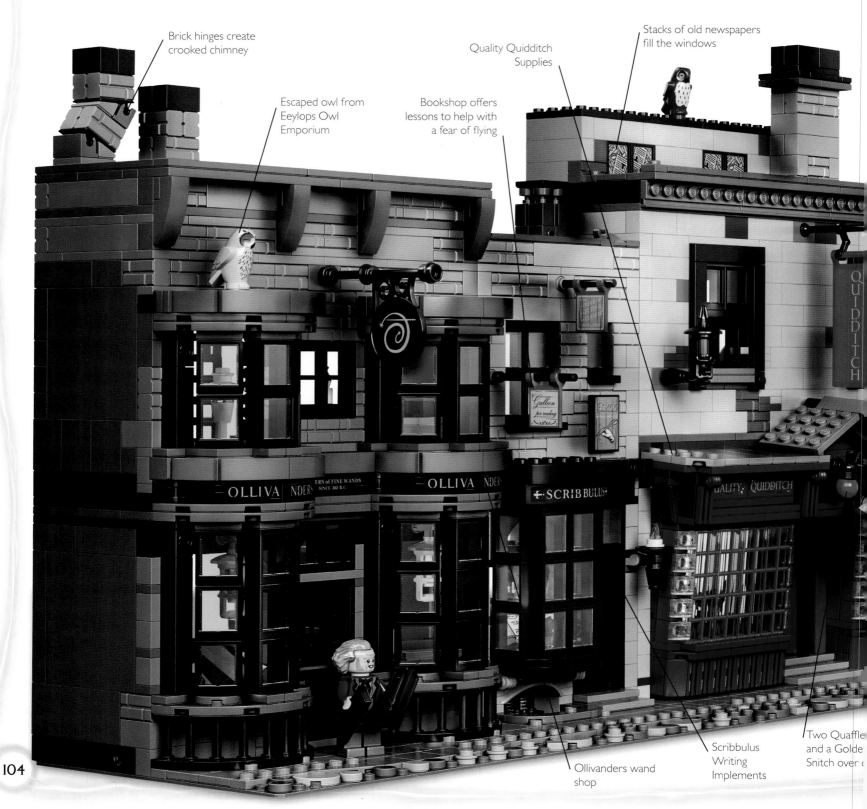

Brick hinges create crooked chimney

Escaped owl from Eeylops Owl Emporium

Quality Quidditch Supplies

Bookshop offers lessons to help with a fear of flying

Stacks of old newspapers fill the windows

Ollivanders wand shop

Scribbulus Writing Implements

Two Quaffle and a Golde Snitch over

MR. OLLIVANDER

Master wandmaker Garrick Ollivander understands all the intricacies of wandlore. His family have been making and selling fine wands at Ollivanders since 382BCE.

Dapper cravat

Florian Fortescue's Ice-Cream Parlor

Flourish & Blotts displays books outside

Black lipstick pieces appear to support canopy

The Daily Prophet offices

Entrance to Knockturn Alley is through here

SCRIBBULUS

The smell of fresh parchment and newly sharpened quills heralds the start of the new school year at Scribbulus Writing Implements—especially for super-organized Hermione. Here, students stock up on their stationery before September 1.

Darker version of Mr. Ollivander's hair piece

Wafer-inspired pattern on vest

MR. FORTESCUE

Delicious treats await in Florean Fortescue's Ice-Cream Parlor. The confectioner makes the best sundaes this side of the Leaky Cauldron.

FLOURISH & BLOTTS

The crowds flock for an exciting book-signing before the start of Harry's second year. Celebrity wizard and fame-seeker, Gilderoy Lockhart promotes his autobiography, *Magical Me* (now in its 27th week atop *The Daily Prophet* bestseller list!), and his adoring fans swoon.

Weasleys' Wizard Wheezes

2x2 window frames in orange for the first time

Gray hair printed on head

MR. BORGIN

This rather sinister-looking wizard runs Borgin and Burkes—a disreputable shop of Dark artifacts on the shady Knockturn Alley, just off Diagon Alley.

Set name	*Diagon Alley*	
Year 2020	**Number** 75978	
Pieces 5,544	**Minifigures** 14	

DIAGON ALLEY SHOPS

At one end of the popular Diagon Alley is the brightly colored Weasleys' Wizard Wheezes, supplying fun and frivolity for all. Down the other end is Ollivanders, which has been uniting wands with wizards and witches for centuries. In between are more independent retailers with quality goods for all magical needs.

▼ OPEN FOR BUSINESS

Next to the Weasleys' joke shop, an arch leads to Knockturn Alley. Only venture there if you're up to no good. At Flourish and Blotts, you can browse books about everything from dragons to alchemy. Pore over the delicious flavors in Florian Fortescue's Ice Cream Parlor, admire the latest racing brooms at Quality Quidditch Supplies, and replenish your stationery at Scribbulus.

Hat-and-hair piece in one

Bag of Knuts, Sickles, and Galleons

BARGAIN-HUNTER

She might be weighed down with bags of wizard Gold, but this witch is after a bargain. Stern-faced, she doesn't want to be ripped off.

Acid Pops candies

Torso piece shared with Mr. Ollivander

DAPPER SHOPPER

From their matching outfits, it looks like this urbane wizard buys his clothes from the same retailer as Mr. Ollivander.

Set name	Diagon Alley	
Year 2020	**Number** 75978	
Pieces 5,544	**Minifigures** 17	

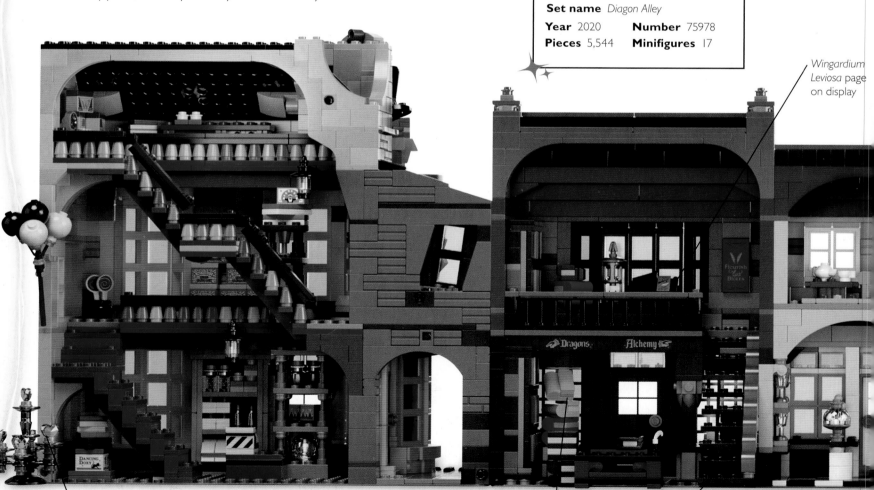

Wingardium Leviosa page on display

Love potions in Weasleys' Wizard Wheezes

Floating books on display in Flourish and Blotts

Staircase folds up

Clean checkered floor in Florian Fortescue's Ice Cream Parlor

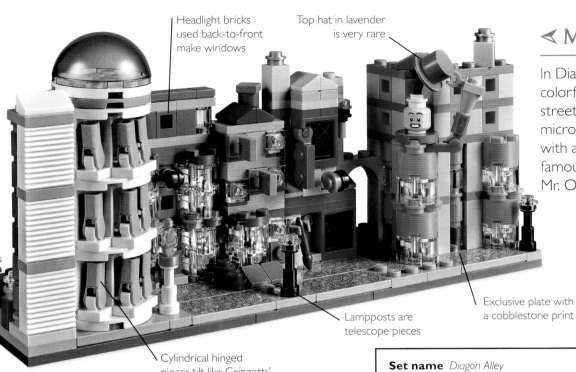

Headlight bricks used back-to-front make windows

Top hat in lavender is very rare

◀ MICROSCALE

In Diagon Alley (set 40289) from 2018, small, colorful pieces capture the variety of the street's architecture. The shops are built in microscale, and the street-scene set comes with a minifigure of Diagon Alley's most famous shopkeeper, the wandmaker, Mr. Ollivander.

Cylindrical hinged pieces tilt like Gringotts' wonky columns

Lampposts are telescope pieces

Exclusive plate with a cobblestone print

Set name	Diagon Alley	
Year 2018	**Number** 40289	
Pieces 374	**Minifigures** 1	

BRICK FACTS

Ollivanders' quality wands come in individual wand boxes. The lower part is a hollow, textured element first introduced in this set. A 1x3 tile clips on top as the lid.

Non-customer facing areas aren't cleaned as often

Storage room for *The Daily Prophet* newspaper

Battered armchair in cozy flat above shop

Chimney stacks have warped with age

FEEL FREE TO TEST-FLY ANY OF OUR BROOMS

Mannequin's torso wears Hufflepuff Quidditch robes

Robes in each House color in Quality Quidditch Supplies

Shelves of quills in Scribbulus

Ollivanders' staircase folds in

WEASLEYS' WIZARD WHEEZES

Roll up! Roll up! Come to Weasley's Wizard Wheezes for some disastrous delights! Weasley twins Fred and George present masterpieces of modern magic in their entertaining joke shop on Diagon Alley. With Dungbombs, Extendable Ears, indoor fireworks, Dancing Doxies, and more, there's always a wheeze guaranteed!

Perches for owls to rest between jobs

Rabbit revealed when top hat lifts up

Hinged arms doff hat

Advert for Skiving Snackboxes

Signs for wizarding shops for robes, pets, and candies

3x3 tile Owl Post sign

Golden owl piece welcomes post

➤ SHENANIGANS FOR ALL!

Flamboyant Fred and George make a statement with their eye-catching shop front. Bright orange and purple with a moving wizard model, it attracts customers from far and wide. The set also includes the Post Office—a site for Owl Post.

Door opens to a drop-off counter

Cobbled street of Diagon Alley

Orange curved window pieces

Either side of the building can attach to the Post Office

BEST FOOT FORWARD

Fred and George have spent years driving their parents up the wall. Now they sell shoes for anyone wanting to walk up the side of a room. With Sticky Trainers on your feet, you can see what it's like to walk like an Acromantula. You'll be climbing the walls in no time!

Face looks too sick for school

Temporary vomiting is convincing enough to fool teachers

▲ FREE PASS FROM CLASS

Puking Pastilles, as advertised here, are the centerpiece of Fred and George's clever Skiving Snackboxes. Those who want to get out of lessons also have the choice of Fainting Fancies, Nosebleed Nougat, and Fever Fudge.

BRICK FACTS

Fancy flying a Frisbee? Fred and George's Fanged Frisbee could be just what you need on your shopping list. The snarling, sharp-toothed toy is a 2x2 round LEGO tile.

▼ TREASURE TROVE

Weasleys' Wizard Wheezes is an assault on the senses—jam-packed with magical money-spinners in an array of dazzling colors. The shop's very popular with students stocking up for the new school year, like Lavender Brown and Romilda Vane.

Matching suits save for colored details

"W" shop logo on tie

THE BEST IN JESTING

Fred and George didn't thrive academically at Hogwarts, but their creativity, practical skills, and rebellious nature are perfect for creating a successful joke shop. The savvy entrepreneurs and ingenious inventors create many of their own products—and test them on themselves!

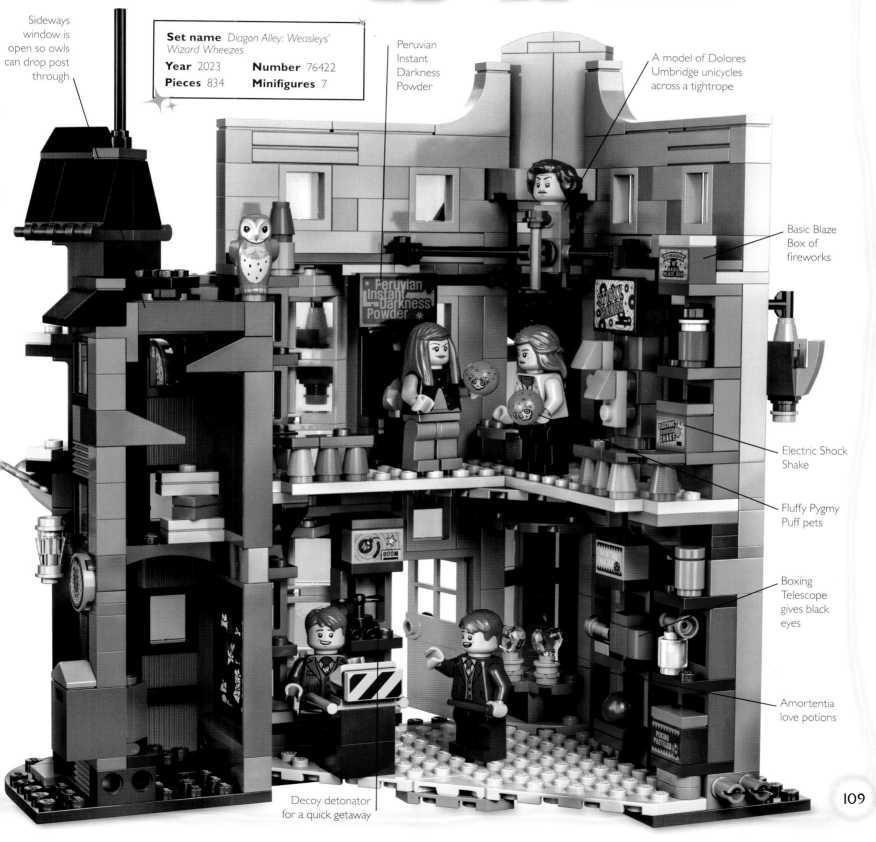

Sideways window is open so owls can drop post through

Set name	*Diagon Alley: Weasleys' Wizard Wheezes*	
Year 2023		**Number** 76422
Pieces 834		**Minifigures** 7

Peruvian Instant Darkness Powder

A model of Dolores Umbridge unicycles across a tightrope

Basic Blaze Box of fireworks

Electric Shock Shake

Fluffy Pygmy Puff pets

Boxing Telescope gives black eyes

Amortentia love potions

Decoy detonator for a quick getaway

GRINGOTTS WIZARDING BANK

Founded in 1474, there's no safer place to store gold than Gringotts. The grand, goblin-run bank has deep underground tunnels and many layers of both physical and magical protections. As Hagrid says, "you'd be mad to try and rob it." The bank's LEGO model stands over 30 in (75 cm) tall, and the above-ground section can be attached to shops in Diagon Alley (set 75978).

Set name
Gringotts Wizarding Bank—Collectors' Edition

Year 2023
Number 76417
Pieces 4,803
Minifigures 13

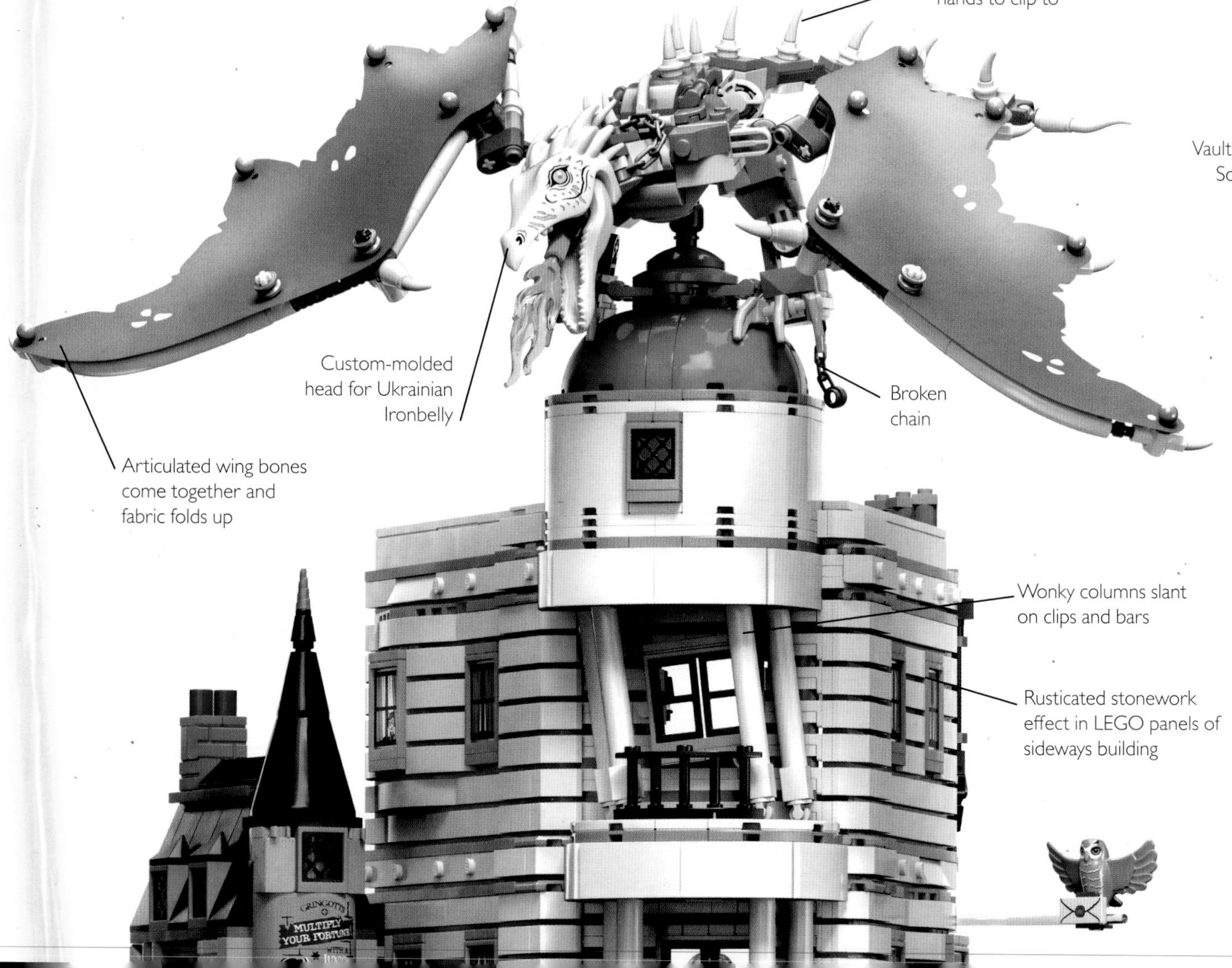

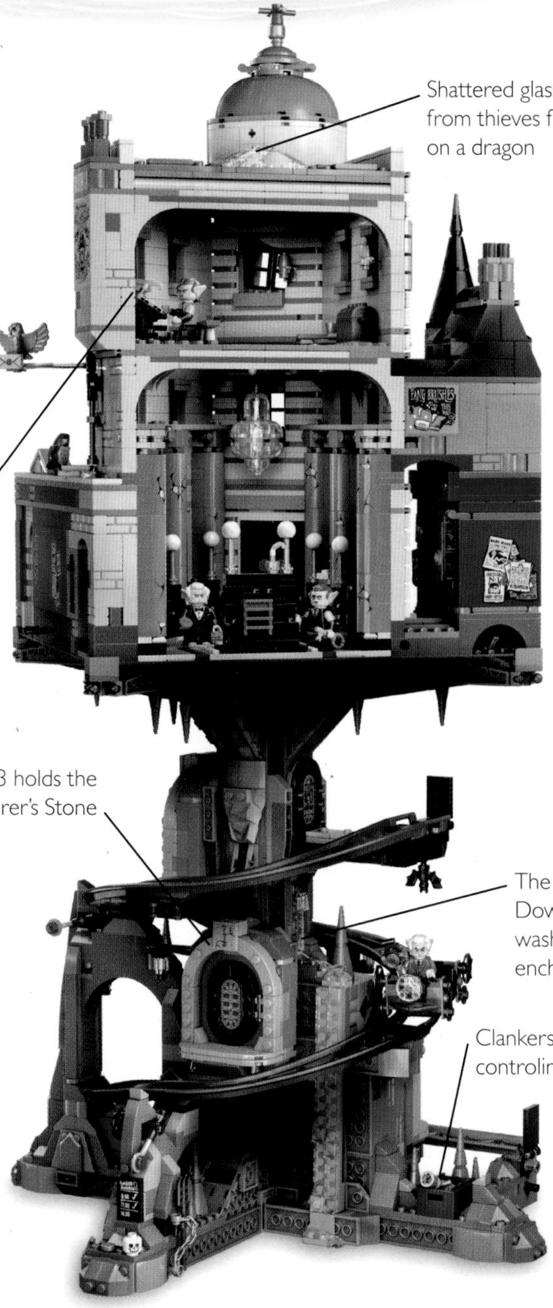

Shattered glass from thieves fleeing on a dragon

Cupboard with top-secret letter from Dumbledore

The Thief's Downfall washes away enchantments

Clankers for controling dragons

Vault 713 holds the Sorcerer's Stone

A SAFE KEEPING

Inside Gringotts, customers are welcomed into a grand foyer with marble columns and a dazzling chandelier. Rows of goblins sit at tall counters. Deep below ground are the vaults in long tunnels accessed via carts that only the goblins can operate. There's also space for the dragon that can otherwise sit atop the model's domed roof.

Many spikes for minifigures' hands to clip to

Broken chain

Wonky columns slant on clips and bars

Rusticated stonework effect in LEGO panels of sideways building

Custom-molded head for Ukrainian Ironbelly

Articulated wing bones come together and fabric folds up

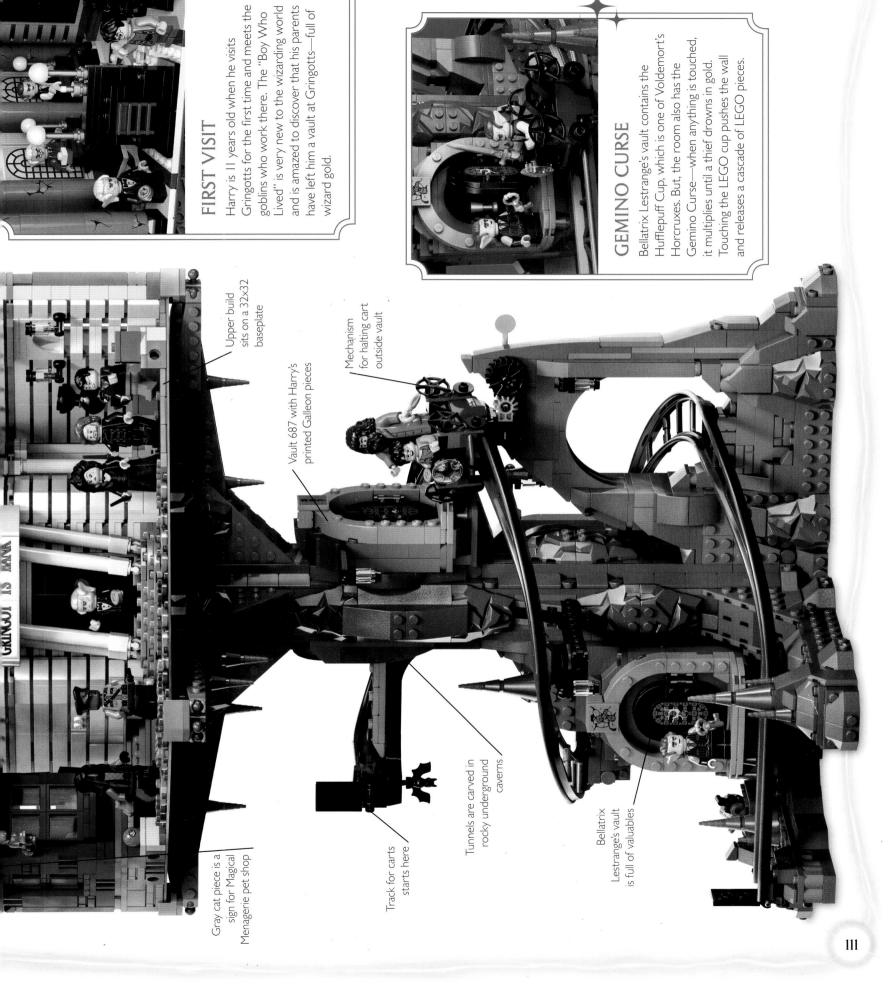

FIRST VISIT

Harry is 11 years old when he visits Gringotts for the first time and meets the goblins who work there. The "Boy Who Lived" is very new to the wizarding world and is amazed to discover that his parents have left him a vault at Gringotts—full of wizard gold.

GEMINO CURSE

Bellatrix Lestrange's vault contains the Hufflepuff Cup, which is one of Voldemort's Horcruxes. But, the room also has the Gemino Curse—when anything is touched, it multiplies until a thief drowns in gold. Touching the LEGO cup pushes the wall and releases a cascade of LEGO pieces.

Upper build sits on a 32x32 baseplate

Mechanism for halting cart outside vault

Vault 687 with Harry's printed Galleon pieces

Gray cat piece is a sign for Magical Menagerie pet shop

Track for carts starts here

Tunnels are carved in rocky underground caverns

Bellatrix Lestrange's vault is full of valuables

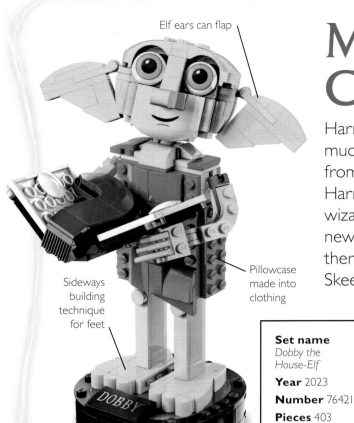

Elf ears can flap

Pillowcase made into clothing

Sideways building technique for feet

DOBBY

MAGICAL COMMUNITY

Harry and his friends are away at school for much of the year, but they aren't cut off from the outside world. As he grows older, Harry meets many members of the wider wizarding community. Some are welcome new friends like the house-elf, Dobby. But there are others, like the reporter Rita Skeeter, who Harry would rather avoid!

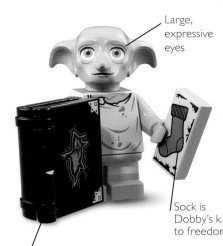

Large, expressive eyes

Sock is Dobby's k[...] to freedo[...]

MINI MINIFIGURE

Dobby's minifigure wears a printed threadbare pillowcase. His house-elf bald head with batlike ears is made from rubbery plastic, but he has a regular torso and short-leg pieces.

Tom Riddle's diary has damage from a Basilisk fang

Set name
Dobby the House-Elf
Year 2023
Number 76421
Pieces 403
Minifigures None

◣ DOBBY

House-elves are usually bound to serve a wizard family by magic that can only be broken by giving the elf clothes. But Dobby is a free elf thanks to Harry Potter. Harry tricks Lucius Malfoy into giving Dobby a sock hidden in a book. Dobby's brick-built model celebrates this moment of liberation.

Classic bowler hat

Office suit under long coat

➤ CORNELIUS FUDGE

As Minister for Magic, Cornelius Fudge could be enjoying the spoils of office, but Dark influences are disrupting his rule. His minifigure is right to look worried—he can only pretend everything is okay for so long before he loses control of his government.

POPPING IN TO VISIT

Eventually, Harry gets a proper bedroom at the Dursleys' house. It has Gryffindor posters and a photo of his parents. The Dursleys have put bars on the window, but these don't stop Dobby the house-elf from magically appearing on Harry's bed.

MISCARRIAGE OF JUSTICE

Cornelius Fudge is Minister for Magic when Buckbeak the Hippogriff is judged to be dangerous after he's provoked by Draco Malfoy. But Draco's father, Lucius, exerts undue influence on the trial. Fudge arrives at Hogwarts with an executioner to oversee the Hippogriff's sentence of death.

RITA SKEETER

Never let the truth get in the way of a good story—that could be Rita Skeeter's motto. The unscrupulous journalist writes sensationalist articles with the help of her magical Quick-Quotes Quill. Together they spin reads that bear little relation to real events.

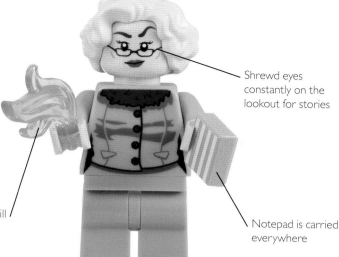

Shrewd eyes constantly on the lookout for stories

Quick-Quotes Quill

Notepad is carried everywhere

Old-fashioned flash on magical camera

Combined wizard hat-and-hair piece

◄ PHOTOGRAPHER

However exciting and outrageous Rita Skeeter's articles are, they sell even more copies when they're illustrated. *The Daily Prophet* photographer takes pictures for the paper. His images move and even wave to readers, but they don't answer back like some paintings do.

PHOTO OPPORTUNITY

The Daily Prophet photographer is sent on location to cover a book-signing in Diagon Alley (set 75978). He gets a bonus photo of the author, Gilderoy Lockhart, with the Boy Who Lived—Harry Potter. But one is keener on being snapped than then other.

Sword of Gryffindor was made by goblins

Large goblin ear is molded to hair piece

GRIPHOOK

The goblin Griphook tolerates wizards and witches, though their two races have a difficult relationship. Goblins have a strong moral code which often clashes with that of wandcarriers. He helps Harry, but very much on his own terms.

IN SAFE HANDS

Thanks to their skills with money, goblins own and run Gringotts Wizarding Bank. Harry meets Griphook there on his first day in Diagon Alley. The goblin takes him to his vault, 687, where Harry discovers the fortune left to him by his parents.

Key for Bellatrix Lestrange's vault at Gringotts

THE KNIGHT BUS

Welcome to the Knight Bus—emergency transport for the stranded witch or wizard. Magical folk stick out their wands at the kerbside and in moments, this towering purple bus will appear and take them wherever they want to go. It provides a fast service, but not a smooth one. Minifigures had better hold on to their hats and hair pieces—they're in for a bumpy ride!

➤ MAGIC BUS

Built in the style of an old-fashioned London bus, but with an extra third deck, the Knight Bus has been on the road since 1865. The bus adapts to the space available, squeezing itself through narrow gaps and bending around tight corners. Equally adaptable, one side of the LEGO model hinges open for easy access.

Set name	*The Knight Bus*	
Year 2019	**Number** 75957	
Pieces 403	**Minifigures** 3	

BRICK FACTS

The striking, high-tech, magical Knight Bus model combines innovation with classic LEGO bricks. Minifigures have been driving LEGO vehicles with steering wheels like this one for decades.

Large headlights for nighttime driving

KNiGHT BUS

OLD 71?

Even the hubcaps are purple!

Roof lifts off easily

3x3 window frame is a
brand-new LEGO piece

BON VOYAGE!

The bus has seats for daytime travel and beds for night journeys. This LEGO bus features a bed on rails so it slides up and down as the bus lurches. Luckily, minifigures aren't at risk of falling out of bed thanks to the brick-built covers. An elaborate chandelier swings from its fitting as the bus bumps along.

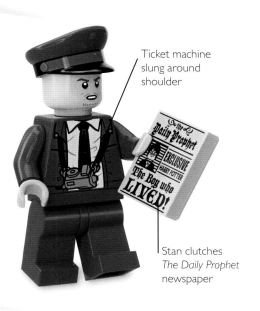

Ticket machine slung around shoulder

Stan clutches *The Daily Prophet* newspaper

ALL
DESTINATIONS
(NOTHING UNDERWATER)

Stan holds onto the pole at the rear entrance of the bus

◄ STAN SHUNPIKE

With a uniform as purple as the bus he works on, Stan Shunpike is the conductor. In Harry's third year at Hogwarts, Stan sells Harry a ticket to travel from his home in Privet Drive to the Leaky Cauldron pub. A ticket to any destination costs 11 sickles, or 13 sickles including hot chocolate—but don't spill it!

Bald patch and white hair are a single piece

➤ ERNIE PRANG

Elderly, white-haired wizard Ernie Prang is the driver of the Knight Bus. He wears large, thick glasses to help him see the road. Ernie also gets a running commentary of what lies ahead from the shrunken head that dangles next to his seat.

Base is built very low to the ground for stability

HOGSMEADE

Near Hogwarts school is the picturesque village of Hogsmeade. It's rare because it's a purely magical settlement—no Muggles know about its existence. At regular points in the school calendar, students from Hogwarts are allowed to Hogsmeade for weekend visits—if they have a signed permission slip from their parent or guardian.

HAPPY HOUR

Harry and Dean Thomas enjoy a quiet drink at the Three Broomsticks on a trip out from school. They drink Butterbeer with a white stud added on top for extra foam. Other refreshment options include Pumpkin Juice and—for adults only—FireWhisky.

➤ WINTRY HIGH STREET

Two establishments on Hogsmeade High Street that are particularly popular with students are Honeydukes sweet shop and the Three Broomsticks pub. In Harry's third year, there's a weekend trip during winter, when snow lies in drifts on the ground and dusts the roofs of the quaint buildings. Harry uses a secret passageway that leads from Hogwarts to Honeydukes.

SWEET SPOT

Cauldron Cakes, Chocolate Frogs, Pumpkin Pasties, Acid Pops, and Bertie Bott's Every Flavor Beans... Honeydukes has it all! Whenever Hogwarts students are let out of school, they fill the candy shop, buying up as many supplies as they can afford, hoping they'll last until the next visit.

Asymmetrical chimneys add to ancient character

Attic room has a cozy fireplace

Chocolate fountain in window display

Set name	*Hogsmeade Village Visit*
Year	2021
Number	76388
Pieces	851
Minifigures	7

LOCAL GRAPEVINE

Hogwarts teachers enjoy a trip into Hogsmeade as much as the students do. Professor McGonagall catches up with gossip in the Three Broomsticks. But in Harry's third year, the news is not good: Sirius Black has escaped from Azkaban. He's believed to be dangerous—and is likely to come after Harry.

Upside-down shield element fronts apex of roof

Three Broomsticks logo

Sheepskin-lined jacket for snowy weather

MADAM ROSMERTA

The landlady of the Three Broomsticks, Madam Rosmerta is a popular and friendly face behind the bar.

Lavender hat is exclusive to Mr. Flume

Candy pattern on poncho

MR. FLUME

Ambrosius Flume runs Honeydukes with his wife. They manage the shop as well as making many of the confectionery products themselves.

MRS. FLUME

Mrs. Flume wears a money belt for the shop's takings. She and her husband also supply the Honeydukes Express trolley aboard the Hogwarts train.

...wy plates can be removed for a year-round look

THE ORDER OF THE PHOENIX

A generation ago, during the First Wizarding War, Albus Dumbledore founded a secret society to lead the fight against the Dark Lord. When it's clear that Voldemort has returned and is recruiting again, the group reforms. With Dark forces infiltrating the Ministry of Magic, the Order must then take matters into their own wand-wielding hands.

Young Fawkes, soon after being reborn

Rubies decorate Sword of Gryffindor

➤ SPARK OF GENIUS

Albus Dumbledore is well placed to lead the Order of the Phoenix. As well as being an incredibly powerful wizard, he knew Voldemort as the child Tom Riddle, so he has a good understanding of how the Dark Lord thinks—which is the key to defeating him.

Pinky purple hair—for now!

Asymmetrical style

ANIMAL ANTICS

As a Metamorphmagus, Tonks can change her appearance at will. She often alters her hair color—either for fun or to express her emotions. Always the entertainer, Tonks captivates Order members at dinner with a pig snout and a duck's bill.

Undone button matches scruffy tie

⌃ FORMER AUROR

Nymphadora, who goes by her surname "Tonks," is a highly skilled Auror—Dark wizard hunter. She trained with the Ministry but no longer trusts it and now works with the Order. Her cheerfulness is expressed in two face prints: a mischievous smile and an entertaining pig snout.

➤ VOICE OF REASON

Wise, intelligent Remus Lupin struggles to be accepted by the wizarding community because of his "furry little problem" of being a werewolf. However, the Order embraces him as a second family. It also provides him with a real family—his wife Tonks.

◄ MINISTRY INSIDER

An accomplished Auror, Kingsley Shacklebolt still works for the Ministry. Usefully, he can keep the Order updated on the Ministry's moves, while also feeding the Minister false information. Working as a mole requires a cool head and Occlumency skills so no one can read his mind.

Nigerian-inspired wizard clothes with agbada ceremonial robe

Casual shirt for being stuck indoors

► RISK-TAKER

Unlike three of his minifigures, Sirius Black has had the chance to shower and put on clean clothes after escaping Azkaban. Harry's godfather is passionate about the Order, but that leads him to take undue risks which are particularly dangerous when he's still wanted by the Ministry.

Floral house robes worn at the Order's headquarters

◄ MATRIARCH

Don't underestimate Molly Weasley. She keeps the domestic wheels of the Order turning, but she's also a brave, powerful witch with a lot to offer in battle. She worries about her children joining the Order, but it's even worse when Percy rejects it and aligns himself with the wayward Ministry.

∨ TENACIOUS

A key member of the Order along with his wife Molly, Arthur Weasley is injured in the line of duty. Voldemort's snake, Nagini, attacks him while he's on guard duty at the Ministry's Department of Mysteries, protecting a mysterious object. Thankfully, Harry realizes and Arthur's life is saved just in time.

Briefcase for office job

∧ THE NEXT GENERATION

Once Fred and George are of age (which is 17 in the wizarding world), they can join in with Order business. Ron, Harry, and Hermione have longer to wait before they're inducted into the Order's secrets. The Weasley twins minifigures in the Order HQ are the same except for their mischievous face prints.

Creepy skull surveys street

Neighboring houses slide apart

12 GRIMMAULD PLACE

Once the grand family home of the Noble and Most Ancient House of Black, number 12 Grimmauld Place fell into disrepair after the last remaining family member, Sirius Black, was wrongly imprisoned. After 12 years, he escapes, and the house becomes the Headquarters for the Order of the Phoenix. It's invisible to Muggles and secure against magical intruders.

Georgian architectural style from 18th-century Britain

SAFE AS HOUSES

Magically concealed on a London residential square of terrace houses, number 12 is hidden between two Muggle houses.

▲ HOME FROM HOME

Number 12 emerges when the houses each side slide apart (without the Muggle residents noticing!) The LEGO house pops out the same way. Harry stays here in the summer and during Christmas of his fifth year at Hogwarts.

Clean, nonprison clothing

Perpetual cranky expression

Molded mouth

◄ GENEROUS LANDLORD

Having inherited the house from his parents, Sirius offers it to the Order. Providing a safe meeting place is very useful, but he's frustrated he can't do more for the cause. He feels trapped in the gloomy house, but going out on missions is too risky. If spotted, he could be sent back to Azkaban—or worse.

➤ KREACHER

A cantankerous, old house-elf, Kreacher comes with the house but is loyal to the old Black family, despite serving Sirius. He does not like his new master or the Order, and no amount of muttering to himself improves his bad temper.

DISGRACED SON

Sirius took a drastically different path from the rest of his wealthy, pure-blood family who were Death Eaters or Death Eater sympathizers. When Sirius ran away to live with James Potter's family, they disowned him, and his mother even burnt him off the Black family-tree tapestry.

DISLOYAL SERVANT

Kreacher absorbed all the Black family's prejudices and beliefs about pure-blood superiority. The rude, unpleasant house-elf is magically bound to serve Sirius, but his true loyalty lies elsewhere so it's wise to be careful about what he overhears. However, perhaps all he really needs is a little kindness?

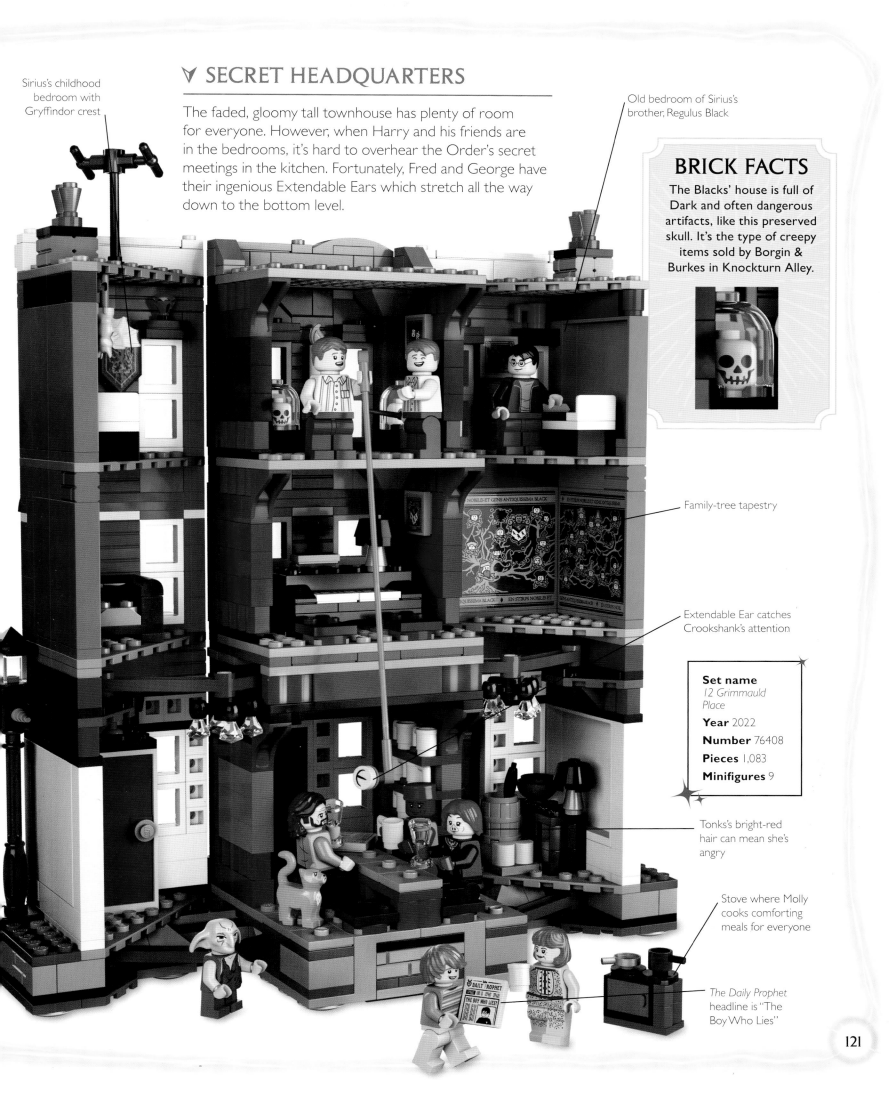

Sirius's childhood bedroom with Gryffindor crest

⊻ SECRET HEADQUARTERS

The faded, gloomy tall townhouse has plenty of room for everyone. However, when Harry and his friends are in the bedrooms, it's hard to overhear the Order's secret meetings in the kitchen. Fortunately, Fred and George have their ingenious Extendable Ears which stretch all the way down to the bottom level.

Old bedroom of Sirius's brother, Regulus Black

BRICK FACTS

The Blacks' house is full of Dark and often dangerous artifacts, like this preserved skull. It's the type of creepy items sold by Borgin & Burkes in Knockturn Alley.

Family-tree tapestry

Extendable Ear catches Crookshank's attention

Set name
12 Grimmauld Place

Year 2022

Number 76408

Pieces 1,083

Minifigures 9

Tonks's bright-red hair can mean she's angry

Stove where Molly cooks comforting meals for everyone

The Daily Prophet headline is "The Boy Who Lies"

THE MINISTRY OF MAGIC

Just like the Muggle world, the wizarding community is run by a central government. The Ministry of Magic is there to keep witches and wizards safe, overseeing magical law and order and aspects of daily life such as education, transportation, safety regulations, and international and Muggle relations.

⌄ OFFICE BLOCK

Hundreds of witches and wizards work for the Ministry of Magic. The bureaucrats spend their day in the vast offices in a secret location, somewhere below central London. The underground many-storied building is a bustling hive of activity, and the set comes with six rooms.

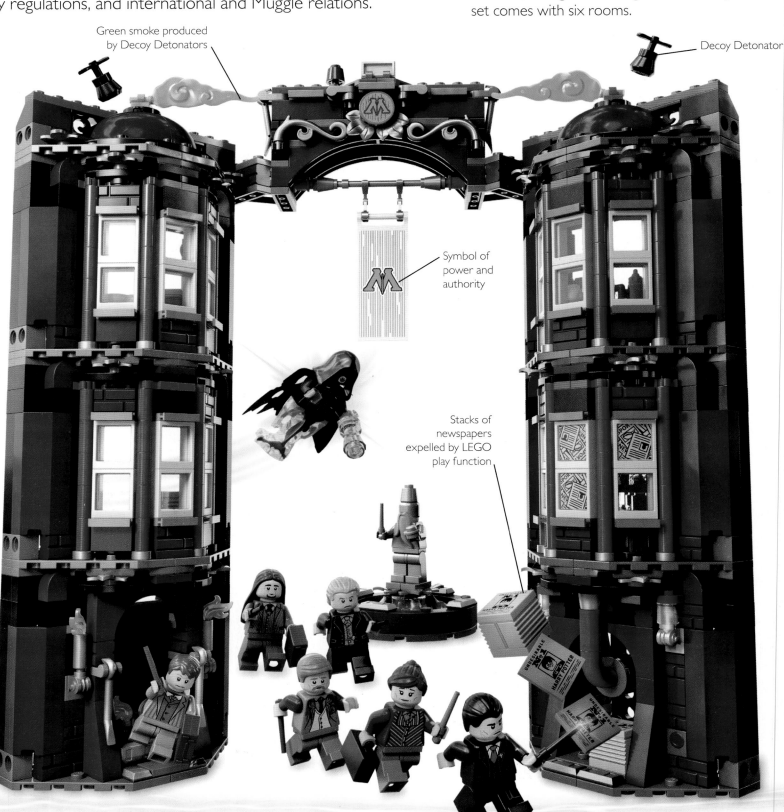

Green smoke produced by Decoy Detonators

Decoy Detonator

Symbol of power and authority

Stacks of newspapers expelled by LEGO play function

Printed door panel

◄ VISITOR ENTRANCE

On an ordinary London street is an unassuming phone box that Muggles stream past every day. It carries visitors down into the bowels of the Ministry, into the gleaming, tiled atrium.

COMMUTING

Instead of using the visitor entrance, employees use the Floo Network. With a green flash, they arrive in one of the many fireplaces that line the Ministry's halls. This LEGO entrance has a play feature so minifigures appear, as if by magic!

ARTHUR'S OFFICE

Mr. Weasley works in the Misuse of Muggle Artifacts Office. He has a particular interest in Muggles objects and is determined to understand how planes, clocks, and rubber ducks work. On the wall, his family watches over him from a photo of their vacation in Egypt.

Decorative LEGO ingot pieces

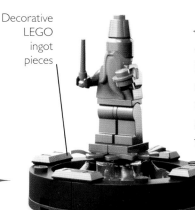

◄ MONUMENT TO MAGIC

In the central atrium of the Ministry, gold statues and a water fountain celebrate the rule of law. A shining minifigure with a long beard and wizard hat holds aloft a golden wand and an orb. He stands on a plinth of transparent flowing water surrounded by golden frogs.

▻ DEADLY PAPER PUSHER

After her stint at Hogwarts, Dolores Umbridge returns to the Ministry, more self-important than ever. Promoted from being the Minister's Senior Undersecretary, she's now Head of the Muggle-Born Registration Commission and has the power to send innocent people to Azkaban.

Pale-pink cat stole

DOLORES'S OFFICE

Installed back in her office at the Ministry, Umbridge sits surrounded by gaudy pink and her mewling cat plates. Important departmental documents pile up on her ornate desk—along with a printed tile of Slytherin's locket.

Set name
The Ministry of Magic

Year 2022

Number 76403

Pieces 990

Minifigures 12

BRICK FACTS

Previously used on signposts, this LEGO element is now an inter-departmental memo. Flying paper-plane messages are far less messy than the owls the Ministry used to use.

HALL OF PROPHECY

Deep in the Department of Mysteries are shelves lined with prophecies, like a filing cabinet of glowing spheres. But be careful: glass orbs are fragile and the whole LEGO shelf unit can fall over.

MINISTERIAL STAFF

The Ministry of Magic has fallen! Voldemort has seized control and put his Death Eaters in charge of the wizarding world's government that affects all aspects of life. The Ministry's motto is now "Magic is Might" and it's turning society from a temple of tolerance to a place where wizards and witches turn on each other in a climate of fear, injustice, and despair.

Wand is not under Thickness's control

Ministry pin

➤ PUPPET MINISTER

It's hard to say whether Pius Thicknesse would be a good Minister for Magic or not, because he's under the illegal and Unforgivable Imperius Curse. This means he can't think for himself and is being controlled by Voldemort, whether he likes it or not. He was installed by the Dark Lord after the previous Minister was attacked by Death Eaters.

Umbridge sits at an intimidating height over defendants

Register of Muggle-borns

Slytherin's locket is a Horcrux

Umbridge's Patronus protects her from Dementors guarding the court

Set name	The Ministry of Magic	
Year 2022	**Number** 76403	
Pieces 990	**Minifigures** 12	

Mary Cattermole's expression reveals the terror she faces

◄ BLOOD STATUS TRIALS

All employees are now subjected to an evaluation to determine their blood status. Anyone deemed undesirable is imprisoned in Azkaban—or worse. Dolores Umbridge is thrilled by the idea of judging her fellow wizards and witches. As Head of the Muggle-born Registration Commission, she holds unfair hearings in the Ministry court room.

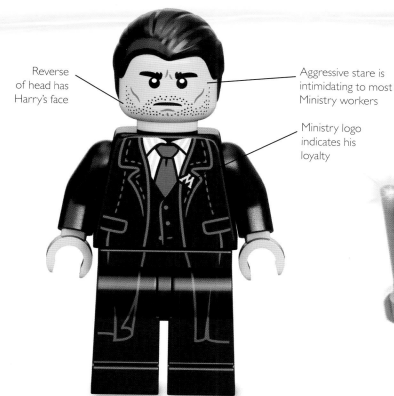

Reverse of head has Harry's face

Aggressive stare is intimidating to most Ministry workers

Ministry logo indicates his loyalty

Hair tied up for work

Alternative face print is Hermione's

Hermione's wand

⊼ ALBERT RUNCORN

When Harry, Hermione, and Ron infiltrate the Ministry to retrieve Slytherin's locket from Dolores Umbridge, they use Polyjuice Potion to take the personas of employees. Harry makes a good choice: Albert Runcorn is a powerful Muggle hunter. Very few people in the Ministry dare challenge his authority.

⊼ MAFALDA HOPKIRK

This is what Mafalda Hopkirk looks like on her way to work, but in this set she's actually Hermione in disguise. As an assistant in the Ministry's Misuse of Magic Office, Mafalda would surely have something to say about this misapplication of Polyjuice Potion!

Troubled brow because his wife, Mary, is on trial

Rain from Yaxley's office

◀ REG CATTERMOLE

An employee in the Ministry's Magical Maintenance Department, Reg Cattermole has tasks like keeping the building in order and stopping the rain that's been falling for two days in Corban Yaxley's office. The pressure is on for Ron, who is posing as Reg— Yaxley has control over Reg's wife's hearing about her blood status.

BRICK FACTS

Harry is now the Ministry's Undesirable No. 1 with a bounty on his head of 10,000 Galleons. The Ministry churns out thousands of leaflets like this one on a 2x2 tile.

THE ROOM OF REQUIREMENT

Dumbledore's Army aren't the only ones who know about the Room of Requirement. Many years ago, Voldemort used this secret room to hide one of his Horcruxes: the Diadem of Ravenclaw. In order to defeat the Dark Lord, Harry must find and destroy all the Horcruxes. There's no time to lose!

➢ CHANGING ROOMS

The Room of Requirement's shape, size, and purpose vary each time it appears because those factors all depend on the user's needs. That's why this LEGO set is so different from Hogwarts Room of Requirement (set 75966). This version also fits with other modular Hogwarts sets.

Sections are part of the modular Hogwarts system

Blind creature finds prey through magic

Textured cone in sand-green is exclusive to Hogwarts sets

Cornish Pixie

Clear bars for attaching "flying" minifigures on their brooms

Many LEGO® Technic holes so the Fiendfyre can be moved around

Set name	*Hogwarts: Room of Requirement*	
Year 2023		**Number** 76413
Pieces 587		**Minifigures** 5

Fiendfyre rips through the building

◁ WHERE EVERYTHIN IS HIDDEN

Over the years, many people have use the Room for hiding things. From it's ta stacked position, this set can be opene up to allow more space for playing—a fighting the Fiendfyre.

➤ FIENDFYRE

This is no ordinary fire. The sentient flames unleashed on the Room of Requirement are cursed Fiendfyre. It snakes its way through the room with an almighty roar, weaving and winding to hunt its victims and leaving devastation in its wake.

LEGO Technic pins attach to the room's walls

Flaming tail

Basilisk head piece in bright orange

Body sections can join together or to the building

Eyeless face of flames

SLIDING DOORS

Two stone wall-panels slide apart to reveal the doors to the magical Room of Requirement. This only happens when the room is really needed. As Helena Ravenclaw says about accessing the room, "If you have to ask, you'll never know; If you know, you need only ask."

GHOSTLY CLUE

The Lost Diadem of Ravenclaw —a tiara that belonged to Rowena Ravenclaw long ago— has not been seen in living memory. So to track it down, Harry must speak to someone who isn't living. He visits Helena Ravenclaw's ghost and persuades her to share her story. It gives him the clue he needs: the Room of Requirement.

BRICK FACTS

First used in gold as a crown or tiara for princesses, this piece can attach to some character's hair pieces. It appears in silver only as the Diadem of Ravenclaw, and it clips into a transparent display stand.

Cabinet in the Room of Requirement is reminiscent of Draco Malfoy's Vanishing Cabinet

Basilisk fang

◄ THE LOST DIADEM

Finding the Lost Diadem of Ravenclaw, which Voldemort turned into a Horcrux, is one thing, but Harry must destroy it, too. Getting rid of a Horcrux is not straightforward. The very powerful, very dark magic is immune to most usual forms of destruction. A Basilisk fang from the Chamber of Secrets fortunately does the trick. That's another Horcrux down; two to go.

BATTLE OF HOGWARTS

Lightning has struck. Harry is back at Hogwarts and so is Voldemort. After 17 years of gathering strength, he's finally back to fighting form and has a whole army behind him. He makes the staff and students of Hogwarts an offer: hand over Harry Potter and they will be spared. Everyone in the wizarding world takes a side and gets ready to battle.

Double-sided panel shows broken clock and clock intact

Scabior gets a thrill from attacking the school

Set name
The Battle of Hogwarts
Year 2023
Number 76415
Pieces 730
Minifigures 6

Large doors rumble as the castle is attacked

Turrets can be built "broken" or "fixed"

▲ PLAYING FOR TIME

Before Harry faces Voldemort, he needs to find and destroy the Lost Diadem of Ravenclaw, which is a Horcrux. While he does this, the residents of Hogwarts, along with the Order of the Phoenix, hold off the Dark Lord's forces for as long as possible. Magical protective enchantments only last so long; soon everyone is dueling one-on-one.

TRUE GRYFFINDOR

While the battle rages around him, Neville has a crucial task: kill the snake with the Sword of Gryffindor. As a Horcrux, Nagini contains part of Voldemort's soul. Until she's destroyed, Voldemort cannot be defeated—not by the Chosen One or by anyone else.

128

BATTLEGROUND

The modular build of Hogwarts can be connected together in different ways: with the clock tower and doors of the Great Hall as below, or with the ramparts. It can also be built in a battle-damaged derelict way or as it looks before (and after) the destructive fighting.

Dueling blasts

Gleeful Bellatrix is in her element

Triumphant smile

Serpent pendant

VICTORIOUS
Molly Weasley wouldn't normally hurt a fly, but she's fighting for everything she cares about, and she finally puts an end to Bellatrix.

DEFEATED
Bellatrix Lestrange—now with dual-molded arms —runs out of cruel tricks in the battle, and Molly Weasley gets to have the last laugh at her expense.

ULTIMATE SHOW-DOWN

As Sybill Trelawney prophesized 17 years ago about the Dark Lord and Harry Potter, "Either must die at the hand of the other, for neither can live while the other survives." Finally, the time comes for the conclusion to the prophecy that has shaped Harry's life since he was born...

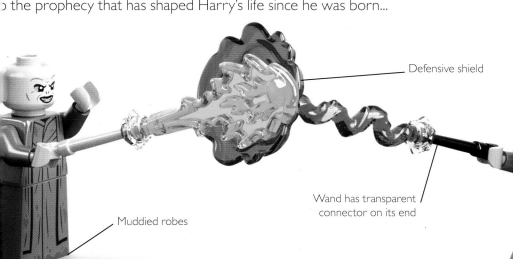

Defensive shield

Wand has transparent connector on its end

Muddied robes

BRICK FACTS
Harry and Voldemort battle with powerful magic, captured in these LEGO pieces. They're new for 2023 but inspired by power blast elements from other LEGO themes.

BEYOND
THE BRICK

LEGO® BRICKHEADZ™

LEGO® Harry Potter™ characters were first transfigured into cuboid LEGO Brickheadz in 2018. This LEGO theme began in 2016, initially turning characters from the LEGO® Marvel and DC™ themes into buildable caricatures using standard LEGO bricks. LEGO Brickheadz now includes a roll call of the wizarding world with witches, wizards, and some Brickheadz that are not even human.

THE BOY WHO LIVED AND HIS OWL
Harry Potter & Hedwig
• 2018 • Set number 41615
•180 pieces

HARRY'S BEST FRIEND
Ron Weasley & Albus Dumbledore
• 2018 • Set number 41621
• 245 pieces

THE BRIGHTEST WITCH OF HER AGE
Hermione Granger • 2018
• Set number 41616 •127 pieces

HOGWARTS HEADMASTER
Ron Weasley & Albus Dumbledore
• 2018 • Set number 41621
• 245 pieces

KEEPER OF KEYS AND GROUNDS AT HOGWARTS
Hagrid & Buckbeak • 2020
• Set number 40412 • 270 pieces

HIPPOGRIFF HERO
Hagrid & Buckbeak
• 2020 • Set number 40412
• 270 pieces

TERRIBLE TRIO
Voldemort, Nagini, & Bellatrix
• 2021 • Set number 40496 • 344 pieces

AWESOME FOURSOME
Harry, Hermione, Ron, & Hagrid • 2021
• Set number 40495 • 466 pieces

SEVERUS SNAPE
Professors of Hogwarts
• 2022 • Set number 40560
• 601 pieces

MINERVA MCGONAGALL
Professors of Hogwarts
• 2022 • Set number 40560
• 601 pieces

SYBILL TRELAWNEY
Professors of Hogwarts
• 2022 • Set number 40560 •
601 pieces

MAD-EYE MOODY
Professors of Hogwarts
• 2022 • Set number 40560
• 601 pieces

GRYFFINDOR SEEKER
Harry Potter & Cho Chang
• 2023 • Set number 40616
• 267 pieces

RAVENCLAW SEEKER
Harry Potter & Cho Chang
• 2023 • Set number 40616
• 267 pieces

SLYTHERIN SEEKER
Draco Malfoy & Cedric Diggory
• 2023 • Set number 40617
• 262 pieces

HUFFLEPUFF SEEKER
Draco Malfoy & Cedric Diggory
• 2023 • Set number 40617
• 262 pieces

KINGSLEY SHACKLEBOLT
Kingsley Shacklebolt & Nymphadora
Tonks • 2023
• Set number 40618 • 250 pieces

TONKS
Kingsley Shacklebolt &
Nymphadora Tonks • 2023
• Set number 40618 • 250 pieces

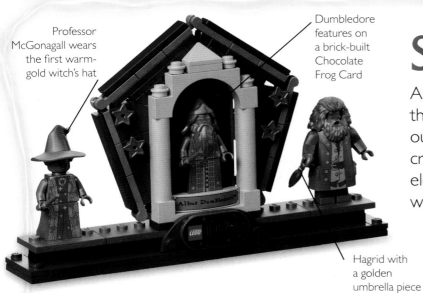

Professor McGonagall wears the first warm-gold witch's hat

Dumbledore features on a brick-built Chocolate Frog Card

Hagrid with a golden umbrella piece

SPECIALIST SETS

As well as recreating the characters, buildings, and scenes from the Harry Potter movies, LEGO designers have also branched out into other types of set inspired by J. K. Rowling's magical creations. There are decorative items, collectable anniversary elements, seasonal offerings, playsets, and customizable sets with which you can make your own mark on LEGO Harry Potter.

⌄ LEGO MOSAICS

In 2021, the LEGO® Art mosaic theme joined forces with the wizarding world to create Harry Potter Hogwarts Crests (set 31201). One set can build any one of the four house crests or a portrait of Hedwig, and four sets combine to make a large school crest. The set also comes with a QR code that links to a podcast to listen to while building.

⌃ 20TH ANNIVERSARY

The first LEGO Harry Potter sets launched in 2001 alongside the theatrical release of the first movie, *Harry Potter and the Sorcerer's Stone*. To celebrate LEGO Harry Potter's 20th anniversary in 2021, nine golden minifigures were created. Each featured as a bonus addition in the sets throughout the year, with three appearing together on this stand from Hogwarts Icons—Collectors' Edition (set 76391).

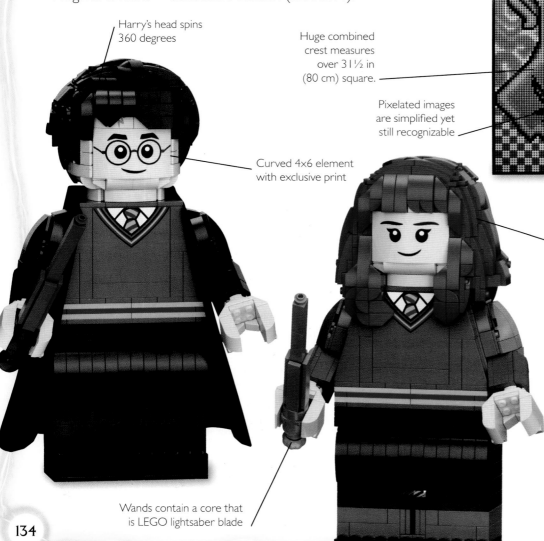

Harry's head spins 360 degrees

Huge combined crest measures over 31½ in (80 cm) square.

Individual images are built on nine panels with 16x16 studs

Curved 4x6 element with exclusive print

Pixelated images are simplified yet still recognizable

Figures are roughly six times the size of regular minifigures

◄ ENGORGIO!

In 2021, LEGO designers supersized Harry Potter & Hermione Granger (set 76393) with 1,673 pieces, appearing to use the Engorgement Charm so the figures stand $10^2/_5$ in (26.5 cm) tall. The models look simple, but complex engineering inside enables the arms, hips, and legs to move in the same way as a regular minifigure's can, and with the correct friction so they can hold their poses.

Wands contain a core that is LEGO lightsaber blade

COUNTDOWN TO CHRISTMAS

[2]019 saw the first LEGO Harry Potter [A]dvent Calender, following a tradition that [h]ad become very popular with the LEGO® [S]tar Wars™ theme. These annual sets [h]ave drawn on Harry's first Christmas [a]t Hogwarts, the Yule Ball, and a snowy [v]isit to Hogsmeade, among other scenes.

The Sorting Hat is 9½ in (24 cm) tall and its brim has a diameter of 7½ in (19 cm)

◀ THE SORTING HAT

In 2024, LEGO fans were able to discover which house they belong to. Just like the Sorting Hat that sits on children's heads to allocate them into houses, this brick-built Sorting Hat can speak! It has a sound brick with 31 randomized sound combinations, which are activated when the model is tipped or put on a real person's head!

Brick-built stand with all four houses represented

Harry hasn't been sorted yet so he wears robes without Gryffindor colors

▼ ALL TO PLAY FOR

Quidditch Trunk (set 76416) from 2023 comes in a trunk that opens out to reveal a Quidditch pitch. The playset has elements that can be customized—along with the score. As well as a named Quidditch player minifigure from each house, there are 10 extra heads and hair pieces in a range of shades for making your own players.

Name plate can be written on

House points tracker

Colors can be customized for a single house

Key locks and unlocks box

Quaffle about to score a goal

Plastic hood collar was new in 2023

Disc shooter for firing Quaffle

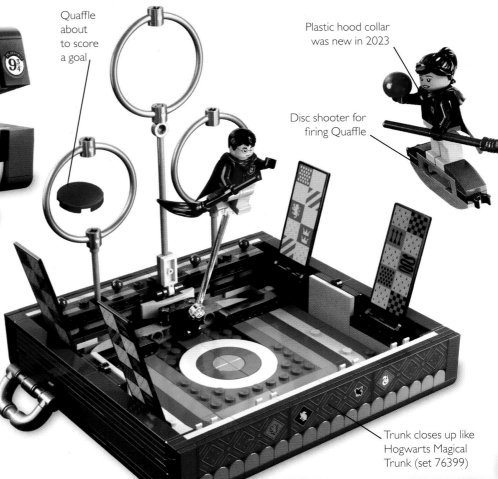

Trunk closes up like Hogwarts Magical Trunk (set 76399)

▲ DESIGN YOUR OWN

[H]ogwarts Magical Trunk (set 76399) from [2]022 is all about customization. It recreates [t]he Sorting Ceremony, the Welcoming Feast, [o]r a common room and dormitory space. 10 [m]inifigure heads in five skin tones and 16 hair [p]ieces can be mixed and matched to make a [y]oung minifigure from each house and one [w]ith a uniform that hasn't been sorted yet.

MEET THE TEAM

All the LEGO® Harry Potter™ sets and minifigures are created by the design team in Billund, Denmark. DK spoke to the current group of LEGO Harry Potter designers to find out how the magic happens.

Above: The LEGO Harry Potter design team in 2023 (Back row from left to right): George Gilliatt, Ina van der Linde, Miriam Toril, Atticus Tsai-McCarthy, Andrew Seenan; (Middle row from left to right): Luna Lund Jensen, Owen Libby, Yi-Chien Cheng, Peter Kjærgaard; (Front row; from left to right): Santiago Andres Carrillo, Jose Julian Rivera Franco, Crisy Dyment, Justin Ramsden.

WHY DO YOU THINK LEGO HARRY POTTER IS SO POPULAR?

First of all, *Harry Potter* itself is super popular, but it also has values that match what LEGO® products are all about. The *Harry Potter* story is about kids being the heroes, their friendships, and their journey together. This all transfers to LEGO bricks really well.

Also, one of the earliest LEGO sets with minifigures was a castle. LEGO bricks have always been great for building these, and Hogwarts is a major part of *Harry Potter*. There are lots of other really interesting locations that make good sets, too, like Diagon Alley and the Shrieking Shack. The set design from the movies is so beautiful to recreate. One of our designers used to be an architect so buildings are very much his thing, and we all refer very closely to the really detailed artwork from the movies. The magical world gives us lots of inspiration.

> *"The Harry Potter story is about kids being the heroes."*

Right: Children, their adventures, and friendships are at the heart of LEGO Harry Potter. These translate brilliantly into LEGO bricks, like in the 2023 Advent Calendar (set 76418).

IS LEGO HARRY POTTER FOR CHILDREN OR ADULTS?

The fan base is quite broad. It's been going for so long now that there are kids who grew up with LEGO Harry Potter 20 years ago who are now introducing their own kids to the world.

So we have fans of lots of different ages. There are kids, older kids, teens, and adults, and we design particular models for the different groups. The characters and places of the movies are the same, of course, but the product experience is normally quite different.

Our models are generally very displayable anyway, but we really focus on what sets are like to display for older fans. The older age group wants something stunning for their shelves, so our focus goes into the beautiful details of these models. For example, we spent a long time discussing the size of the 2023 Hogwarts Castle and Grounds (set 76419) to make sure most people would be able to fit the whole castle and the grounds on their shelf. One of our designers is from Asia, where they grew up in a smaller living space. When he had feedback from a fan that they were going to buy the set because, finally, it would fit on their shelf, the designer was really happy. Then for kids' models, our focus is more on play features and ways to play with the models so kids can use their imaginations.

Right: Beautiful sets for display appeal to older LEGO Harry Potter fans. Hogwarts Castle and Grounds (set 76419) was carefully designed to fit on a shelf.

Left: Sets for younger fans are full of play features. Quidditch Trunk (set 76416) has customizable minifigures, broomsticks to fly, and a shooter that fires the Quaffle at the hoops.

HOW DO YOU DECIDE WHICH SETS AND MINIFIGURES TO MAKE?

Generally the sets come first and then we decide which minifigures to include. There are many reasons why we choose what we do, but overall, we think about our long-term plans and how things will pan out over the coming years.

Some series run for a number of years, like Hogwarts. The castle is likely to be available in some form or another, but we try to keep it new and fresh. For example, we had a series of castle sets running from 2018 to 2020, and then in 2021, we launched the modular castle series. Modular means that each set is a different part of the castle and they can be combined together to make a bigger castle. In 2024, we launched a new and exciting series of sets with the most detailed and authentic minifigure scale version of the castle we've ever done.

Right: The seven modular Hogwarts sets can join together like this, but thanks to their modular assembly they can combine in any number of other ways, too.

76402   76401   76413   76398   76386   76415   76389

Most of our ideas come about during design meetings and discussions. People come up with new ideas or long-forgotten things that someone designed years ago, and we think, "Oh

wow, that actually really fits for launching next year." This year, one of our designers made a model of the second Triwizard Tournament task, just for fun. We'd done a concept model three or four years ago, and it became Triwizard Tournament: The Black Lake (set 76420; see pp. 90–91). We need the right product, but it also has to be the right time. The right time for something might be years after it's first designed.

> *"There are kids who grew up with LEGO Harry Potter 20 years ago who are now introducing their own kids to the world."*

THE STORY HAS FINISHED SO THERE'S NO NEW CONTENT. DOES THAT MAKE YOUR JOB EASIER OR HARDER?

The fact that the *Harry Potter* story has finished has a lot of benefits. It means we can plan a long way ahead, but the challenge, of course, is that we have to reinvent the same characters and places and deliver experiences that are new. We don't want to just copy-and-paste what we've done before.

We've always tried to create new experiences. When we relaunched in 2018, we also did sets for the *Fantastic Beasts* film. One was Newt's Case of Magical Creatures (set 75952). It was a suitcase that opened up in a special way to reveal a scene inside. Since then, we've used this idea in different ways. The LEGO Harry Potter Moments sets are books that open up into classrooms (see pp. 62–66 and 70–71). The House Banner sets open up into commons rooms (see pp. 50–56). And there are Hogwarts Magical Trunk (set 76399) and Quidditch Trunk (set 76416), which are school luggage that open up into scenes (see p. 135). Every so often we have something brand new, like these novelty concepts, which add a bit of excitement.

Below: The 2018 set Newt's Case of Magical Creatures (set 75952) pioneered the idea of enclosing a fun scene within a trunk.

HOW ELSE DO YOU VARY THE CONTENT TO MAKE IT FRESH?

Normally we make play sets that are in the same scale as minifigures, but Dobby the House-Elf (set 76421) and Expecto Patronum (set 76414) are examples where we took classic ideas from *Harry Potter* and then reinvented them by building them at a bigger scale. We've also created Hogwarts Castle in many different scales. All the models are based on the same castle from the movies, but they're designed for different people. We've had Hogwarts as the small polybag set (see below), as play sets and the series of modular builds, then as the big high-price adult microscale build Hogwarts Castle (set 71043; see pp. 36–37), and the even smaller-scale nanoscale build Hogwarts Castle and Grounds (set 76419; see p. 37).

Left: The small polybag set Build Your Own Hogwarts Castle (set 30435) with Dumbledore is an example of how we can take Hogwarts castle and present it in a different way.

Microscale and nanoscale are terms that we use at the LEGO Group. Microscale is too small for minifigures. Instead, it's based around the microfigure, which is a single molded piece originally created as a trophy for a minifigure to hold. Then nanoscale is even smaller. Even a small microfigure would be too big for those sets.

Right: This minifigure from Chinese New Year Temple Fair (set 80105) holds a human-shaped trophy, which has become the microfigure.

HOW LONG DOES IT TAKE TO DEVELOP A MODEL?

That really varies and depends on the size and the type of model. The overall process, from the initial concept to the product being in a shop, generally takes one to two years, but that's not all design time. There are many other tasks to be done. The building instructions need to be created and checked. Any new pieces need to be developed, have test molds made, and go into production. The packaging layouts have to be designed with an image on the box that kids are going to fall in love with. There are a lot of jobs that need to happen before a set hits the shelf.

> *"There are a lot of jobs that need to happen before a set hits the shelf."*

HOW DO YOU DESIGN SETS?

We develop products throughout the year. Sometimes the process is quite organic, though we do have a clear concept phase and a maturing phase, and these connect with processes in other departments in the LEGO Group.

Normally, an idea sparks from one of our design meetings. We very much work together. Ideas are thrown around and then built upon. So it starts from an initial discussion and then a concept model, which gets passed around. We have people who are particularly fast at just creating something, either digitally or with bricks. The concept goes from designer to designer, to get different suggestions for how it could develop. Finally, once we're all happy with the overall direction, the model is assigned to one designer to develop. A graphic designer looks at the prints and stickers, and our element designers look at any new pieces needed. But we still very much work as a team. We're all designers so we all have design opinions and we always help each other out coming up with ideas.

Above: Having figured out the mechanism to make 12 Grimmauld Place move, the designer did this quick drawing to work out the proportions and details in LEGO bricks.

"We're all designers so we all have design opinions and we always help each other out coming up with ideas."

WHAT SETS HAVE YOU DONE THAT WERE PARTICULARLY CHALLENGING?

In 2023, we put out Gringotts Wizarding Bank—Collectors' Edition (set 76417). A lot of teamwork went into that one. When we released the huge Diagon Alley (set 75978) in 2020, it was missing Gringotts Wizarding Bank. Fans were super excited to get that, so we knew we had high expectations to meet. It was a real challenge to make something compatible with the Diagon Alley set. We wanted to include the underground vault section, but it was hard to work out how we could possibly make a building that fits with the rest of the street while standing on top of a giant rock structure. It was also tricky to make the rock look higgledy-piggledy and like it's about to tip over, when really it is incredibly strong and stable.

The set has lots of fun details. The graphic designer worked very closely with element designers to figure out how to create the head for the big Ukrainian Ironbelly dragon. It's a very specific creature that needs to look scary, but in some ways, it's also very sad. We wanted to capture the look of a starved, badly treated dragon, but also make it a child-friendly piece for this awesome set.

For its lower jaw, we used a piece from a LEGO Baryonyx from the LEGO® Jurassic World theme. We share LEGO elements with a lot of the different LEGO teams and work closely together with them.

Above: When developing Gringotts Wizarding Bank—Collectors' Edition (set 76417), the team spent a long time figuring out the layout. When it came to finalizing the look, they made a drawing to iron out the details.

"It was also tricky to make the rock look higgledy-piggledy and like it's about to tip over, when really it is incredibly strong and stable."

Above: It was a challenge to make the Ukrainian Ironbelly dragon seem fierce and dangerous while also being a sorry-looking creature.

Right: This microscale model was built to show how we could make Gringotts with the bank building on top of a giant rock filled with vaults.

Right: For the life-size Galleon coin, a designer hand-drew this sketch to figure out how to translate the Galleon into a LEGO style, taking inspiration from a LEGO dragon element from the 1990s.

Left: There was already a minifigure-scale Galleon coin, but the designers wanted to include a life-size one as a special treat for fans in the Gringotts set.

HOW DO KIDS HELP WITH DESIGNING SETS?

We organize tests where kids come in and play with the sets. It gives us a chance to check the stability of the models and make sure they work as expected. It's useful to see, for example, where and how someone instinctively picks up a model, in case it's not where we expected and we need to adjust the build. For the Gringotts Wizarding Bank—Collectors' Edition (set 76417) we show in the building instructions how to pick the model up because it's so big. We're all LEGO Harry Potter fans ourselves as well, so we test sets on each other, too!

> *"We're all LEGO Harry Potter fans ourselves as well, so we test sets on each other, too!"*

WHAT NEW IDEAS HAS LEGO HARRY POTTER BROUGHT TO LEGO PRODUCTS?

For the House Banner sets, we did something new. The main walls have backgrounds with lenticular prints that show through holes for windows or portraits. Lenticular printing is a technique for printing images on special curved lenses that create images with a sense of depth or that can flick between two images to create the impression of movement. With lenticular printing we could create moving images in the views out of the windows and in portraits on the walls—just like magical moving images in the wizarding world. It was the first time the LEGO Group had used lenticulars in about 20 years. The technology had changed a lot since then. It was quite tricky for us to figure out how to incorporate the semi-3D style of lenticulars with our LEGO style and then bring it all together into the sets. It was a challenge, but it was worth all the hard work.

> *"With lenticular printing we could create moving images—just like in the wizarding world!"*

Left: The lenticular backdrop for Hufflepuff House Banner (set 76412) creates a sense of distance through the windows and has magical moving paintings. In her portrait, Helga Hufflepuff lifts the Hufflepuff cup in triumph!

ARE THERE ANY LEGO PIECES THAT BEGAN IN LEGO HARRY POTTER BUT ARE NOW USED ACROSS LOTS OF THEMES?

The *Harry Potter* wand piece is quite iconic. Of course, it was created for LEGO Harry Potter, but now you can see it in other LEGO sets as well. Never as a wand though, because we try and keep its use as wand exclusive to *Harry Potter*. It's interesting to try and find the piece because it's not that common, but you can find it in other sets, used in unusual ways. It's been used as antennas in the LEGO® Creator Cozy House (set 31139). In LEGO® City Downtown (set 60380), a minifigure uses one as a violin bow, and in some LEGO® NINJAGO® sets, it's used as chopsticks.

Right: In LEGO Creator Main Street (31141), a minifigure plays the drums using a pair of LEGO Harry Potter wand pieces as drumsticks.

Another piece that began with the LEGO Harry Potter team is the bendable medium-sized leg piece used for teenagers. Now it has very wide usage. When the characters are younger, in the first or second years at Hogwarts, their minifigures have the shorter legs, which were first used in LEGO® *Star Wars*™. Then the teenager leg piece is great for us to show those middle year

Harry Potter's wig is also a piece that you'll find in other models outside of *Harry Potter*, but always in a different color. Harry is the only minifigure to have it in black.

Above: LEGO Harry Potter characters, like Draco Malfoy, age and grow over the course of the story. LEGO designers have developed rules about which characters from which year have which legs and also which hair pieces.

> *"We really love reusing pieces in different ways—that's the beauty of the LEGO system."*

CAN YOU TELL US ABOUT THE CHOCOLATE-FROG-INSPIRED WIZARD TILES?

These tiles were a fun feature to celebrate our 20th anniversary of LEGO Harry Potter in 2021. Although our current sets began in 2018, there was a first wave of LEGO Harry Potter sets that ran from 2001 to 2011, so 2021 was the 20th anniversary. A new range of the collectable tiles were released in 2024 with the new Hogwarts Castle series.

The designs are based on the collectable Chocolate Frog cards that come with packets of chocolate in the wizarding world. All the tiles print at once and then fall into one basket so when they're picked up by the packing lines, you never know which one you're going to get. The tiles print together so there's the same quantity of each design and exactly the same chance of getting each one.

We think this is a great addition to sets. We try to keep some surprises for our LEGO fans, but even with the Collectible Minifigure lines and Advent Calendars, fans can look online and find out what's inside, so they are losing the excitement of opening a pack to see the contents. Sometimes you're happy because you were missing the element you've just discovered; sometimes you're sad because it's not the one you wanted. We use these collectable tiles to remind people of this feeling. It also encourages friends to swap if they have duplicates, so it's a nice, social thing, too.

Above: Each of the 2×2 tiles features a notable witch or wizard, like Nicolas Flamel or Newt Scamander, just like the Chocolate Frog cards in the wizarding world. There are 16 collectable tiles in the 2021 range and 14 tiles in the 2024 range.

"We try to keep some surprises for our LEGO fans."

WHAT CAN YOU TELL US ABOUT THE MINIFIGURE THAT COMES WITH THIS BOOK?

It's a great minifigure! It's Cedric Diggory in the second Triwizard task from the *Harry Potter and the Goblet of Fire* movie, when he has to swim for an hour down to the bottom of the Black Lake. Cedric has features that were hard to translate into the minifigure style. In the movie he casts a Bubble Head charm, so we gave him an air bubble on his face. We also added a fun feature to make him a bit more exclusive: we gave him a wrist watch. We print on arms all the time, but this might actually be the first time we've ever done a wrist watch. We do try to make these exclusive minifigures have something quite special.

Left: Dobby the House-Elf (set 76421) has eyebrows made with wheel arches from LEGO car sets, and his mouth is printed on a car bonnet piece. It was first used in this pale pinky-peach color for rose petals in the Botanical Collection Flower Bouquet (set 10280).

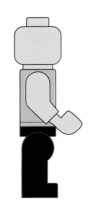

Above: As part of the design process, all LEGO minifigures have digital images made of each side. These images were made for the exclusive Cedric Diggory minifigure that comes with this book.

INDEX

Main entries are highlighted in **bold**.
Sets are listed by their full name.

Number
plate is
gistered to
r. Weasley

7990 TD

Wheels aren't needed
as car is betwitched to fly

Harry's luggage for his
second year at school

Set name
Flying Ford Anglia
Year 2024
Number 76424
Pieces 337
Minifigures 2

Project Editor Nicole Reynolds
Senior Designer Lauren Adams
Designer Thelma-Jane Robb
Production Editor Siu Yin Chan
Senior Production Controller Lloyd Robertson
Managing Editor Paula Regan
Managing Art Editor Jo Connor
Publishing Director Mark Searle

Dorling Kindersley would like to thank Ashley Blais, Randi K. Sørensen, Heidi K. Jensen, Paul Hansford, Martin Leighton Lindhardt, Andrew Seenan, Kerstin Bannert, and the LEGO Harry Potter design team at the LEGO Group; Kurtis Estes, Victoria Selover, and Katie Campbell at Warner Bros. Consumer Products; Luke Barnard from The Blair Partnership; Selina Wood for editorial help; and, at DK, Julia March for index creation.

The author, Elizabeth Dowsett, would like to thank Emily Dowsett for her editorial acumen and her detailed Hermione-like knowledge of everything LEGO Harry Potter.

First American Edition, 2024
Published in the United States by DK Publishing
1745 Broadway, 20th Floor, New York, NY 10019
Previous edition published in 2020 as
LEGO® Harry Potter™ Magical Treasury

Page design copyright © 2024 Dorling Kindersley Limited
DK, a Division of Penguin Random House LLC

24 25 26 27 28 10 9 8 7 6 5 4 3 2 1
001–339318–July/2024

Anglia is a trademark owned and licensed by Ford Motor Company.

A catalog record for this book is available from the Library of Congress.
ISBN: 978-0-7440-9895-2
Library ISBN 978-0-7440-9896-9

DK books are available at special discounts when purchased in bulk for sales promotions, premiums, fund-raising, or educational use. For details, contact: DK Publishing Special Markets, 1745 Broadway, 20th Floor, New York, NY 10019
SpecialSales@dk.com

Printed and bound in China

www.dk.com
www.LEGO.com

This book was made with Forest Stewardship Council™ certified paper—one small step in DK's commitment to a sustainable future. Learn more at www.dk.com/uk/information/sustainability

Your opinion matters

Please scan this QR code to give feedback to help us enhance your future experiences

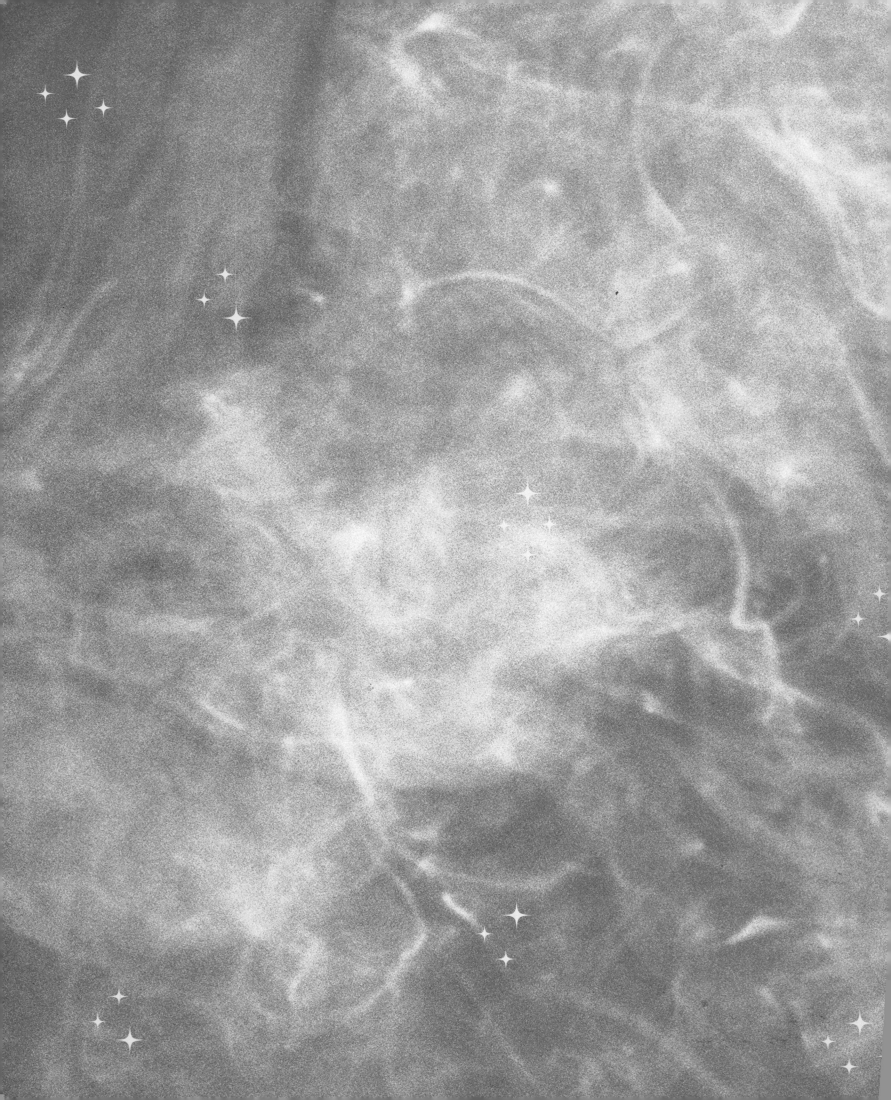